"I'll walk you to your car," Chris said.

There was a moon tonight, and polished stars, and a soft April breeze wafted in from the Cape. Magic stirred inside Tory and, with it, a sweet surge of desire.

Chris walked around to the driver's side. Moonlight shafted across his face, and Tory could see that he looked grave. It struck her anew that he had a great deal to face up to. She wished he'd let her face up to it with him. But he wouldn't.

"Chris..." she began. Before she could say more, he took her in his arms. For a moment he just held her, and she savored the feel of his chest against her. Then he released her, placing a cautionary finger on her lips before she could speak.

"Later" was all he said.

Later. Tory wished she could believe in later.

Dear Reader,

Welcome to the Silhouette **Special Edition**
experience! With your search for consistently
satisfying reading in mind, every month the authors
and editors of Silhouette **Special Edition** aim to offer
you a stimulating blend of deep emotions and high
romance.

The name Silhouette **Special Edition** and the
distinctive arch on the cover represent a
commitment—a commitment to bring you six
sensitive, substantial novels each month. In the
pages of a Silhouette **Special Edition**, compelling
true-to-life characters face riveting emotional
issues—and come out winners. Both celebrated
authors and newcomers to the series strive for depth
and dimension, vividness and warmth, in writing
these stories of living and loving in today's world.

The result, we hope, is romance you can believe in.
Deeply emotional, richly romantic, infinitely
rewarding—that's the Silhouette **Special Edition**
experience. Come share it with us—six times a
month!

From all the authors and editors of Silhouette
Special Edition,

Best wishes,

Leslie Kazanjian,
Senior Editor

MAGGI CHARLES
Strictly for Hire

Silhouette Special Edition

Published by Silhouette Books New York

America's Publisher of Contemporary Romance

To Dick and Barbara Langworth,
with memories of the
New England Chapter of the ASJA.
It was fun while it lasted.

SILHOUETTE BOOKS
300 East 42nd St., New York, N.Y. 10017

ISBN: 0-373-09599-6

First Silhouette Books printing May 1990

All the characters in this book are fictitious. Any
resemblance to actual persons, living or dead, is
purely coincidental.

®: Trademark used under license and
registered in the United States Patent and
Trademark Office and in other countries.

Printed in the U.S.A.

MAGGI CHARLES

wrote her first novel when she was eight and sold her first short story when she was fifteen. Fiction has been her true love ever since. She has written forty-plus romance and mystery novels and many short stories. The former newspaper reporter has also published dozens of articles, many having to do with her favorite avocations, which include travel, music, antiques and gourmet cooking. Maggi was born and raised in New York City. Now she and her writer husband live in a sprawling old house on Cape Cod. They have two sons and two grandchildren.

CAPE COD AND VICINITY

to Boston

Provincetown

25

3

to N.Y. and Ct.

Cape Cod Bay

6

195

6

Sandwich

to R.I.

Bourne

6A

Orleans

Buzzards Bay

6

132

28

Hyannis

28

Falmouth

28

Yarmouth

Chatham

Nantucket Sound

MARTHA'S VINEYARD

Atlantic Ocean

NANTUCKET

Chapter One

March came in like a lion, and by midmonth was still roaring fitfully. Snow threatened both Monday and Tuesday, and on Wednesday, the skies were again congested with swollen charcoal clouds.

It wasn't the kind of day when a person's eyes normally needed protection from the sun. Yet the man sitting stiffly in the rear seat of the pale blue Cadillac Eldorado was wearing dark glasses, and that piqued Tory Morgan's curiosity.

An hour earlier, she had watched him come out of his house, unerringly head for her car, and get in, so there certainly didn't appear to be anything wrong with his eyesight. She suspected both the vintage Caddy and a woman driver had surprised him as much as he'd surprised her. She'd expected Christopher Kendall to be old and ailing, especially since she was chauffeuring him to a Boston hospital complex, a routine run for her from

Cape Cod. As owner and operator of Tory's Limousine Service, she'd soon discovered that trips to Boston area medical facilities ran second only to trips to Logan Airport. Most of her clients were well up in years and preferred to pay for her services rather than cope with heavy traffic themselves.

This client fell into an entirely different category. She placed him in the early to midthirties, and he looked extremely healthy. He was tall, and not only was he built like an athlete—broad-shouldered and narrow-waisted—but he moved like one, too. He was hatless, and his smooth, thick hair was such a dark shade of brown it was almost black. She'd only been able to get a glimpse of his features before he seated himself behind her, but it was a provocative glimpse. The dark glasses shielded enough of his face to make discovering what he actually looked like something of a guessing game. But what she could see made her think of movie idols she'd swooned over as a teenager.

Yes, Christopher Kendall was tall, dark, handsome and, according to local gossip, also rich. So what was his problem?

Curiositie after the affairs of others cannot be without envy and an evil minde.

Tory silently repeated those words written over three centuries ago as the corner traffic light turned from green to red and she slid the long, classic car to a smooth stop.

Jeremy Taylor, in his seventeenth-century tome, *The Liberty of Prophesying*, had been a bit on the grim side. Tory personally disclaimed having an "evil minde," nor was she envious of her passenger. But she was over-whelmingly curious about him.

She glanced in the rearview mirror. Christopher Kendall was staring out the window, but the dark glasses prevented her from reading the expression in his eyes. She sensed, rather than saw, his unhappiness. Melancholy, discontent, tension vibrated from back seat to front seat.

Tory wished she could think of something to say that might ease the atmosphere, but she'd never met any-one more uncommunicative than her present passen-ger. He seemed far too wrapped up in whatever it was that was disturbing him to be easily nudged out of it. She was afraid anything she might say would appear glib or trite or both.

Most of her clients liked to chat, sometimes to the point where their monologues got on her nerves. Christopher Kendall was the extreme opposite. Con-fronting her, back in Chatham, he'd cast an appraising glance at the classic Eldorado then had confirmed the fact that she really *did* represent Tory's Limousine Ser-vice. That settled, she had further set the record straight by adding, "I'm Tory."

At least he'd not accused her of masquerading in a masculine identity as a couple of her earlier customers had. Elderly men, both of them, they'd been disgrun-tled, dyspeptic and had also argued about her charges, even though trip prices were always made raindrop clear before a driving engagement was booked.

Christopher Kendall merely shrugged, then climbed into the back seat of the car. Subsequently, all the way from Chatham to Boston—a distance of ninety-five miles—he had not uttered another word.

The light changed. As the car moved forward, Tory again wished she could come up with something that might splinter the silence. But she couldn't. This man in the back seat, staring tight-lipped out the window, was making her tongue-tied.

She supposed she could ask, "It *is* the Commonwealth Medical Complex you want, isn't it? Not New England Medical Center or Mass General?" But that would merely be an insult to her own intelligence. He'd told her over the phone where he wanted to go. She'd told him how much it would cost him. They had set the time, the place of pickup. He hadn't realized that the person to whom he was speaking on the phone was the same person who would be doing the chauffeuring, that was all. Or that she'd be driving an antique auto. Not that either really had made much difference, or he wouldn't be driving with her now.

Traffic was heavy and getting heavier. Tory was forced to switch her attention away from Christopher Kendall to concentrate totally on the task at hand. Minutes later, she pulled into the semicircular driveway at the Commonwealth Medical Complex, and braked in front of the hospital's wide glass doors.

Her passenger wasted no time in getting out of the car, and he certainly was agile enough. Whatever his problem was, it didn't entail his arms or legs. Over his shoulder he said, "Be back here in two hours, please." Then he was gone before Tory could frame an answer.

She watched him stride toward the medical complex's impressive entrance. He was wearing an expertly tailored cashmere coat, and he walked with the self-assurance of someone used to cutting not just a path but a swathe through life. Tory had been impressed by his home in Chatham, a mini-estate built atop a hill overlooking a beautiful freshwater pond. Now she was also impressed by him. Though life hadn't dealt with her kindly where the male sex was concerned, she had to concede that she was still a romantic at heart. And Christopher Kendall, outwardly at least, was made of the stuff from which romantic, knight-in-armor fantasies are spun. What fun it would be, she thought mischievously, to play Cinderella to his Prince Charming.

Then she sobered. She wished she knew exactly where he was going within the sprawling medical complex. And why he was going there.

Questions about him still tumbled as Tory pulled away from the hospital entrance and headed for a parking garage close to Copley Place. For the next two hours, she wandered through stores such as Neiman Marcus's Boston branch, promising herself as she looked and yearned that one day she'd bring her checkbook with her and splurge. It was a long while since she'd yielded to impulse buying—or, for that matter, to much else that dealt with impulses. Living, just getting from day to day, had become far too pragmatic an affair.

Wandering, she forgot about lunch. And by the time she became aware she was hungry, it was too late to pause for something to eat. As it was, she was caught in a traffic snarl and was several minutes late getting back to the medical complex. She barely had come to a stop in front of the entrance when Christopher Kendall emerged, and she knew she'd kept him waiting.

He was frowning. He looked grim as he got into the back seat, and Tory waited for a tirade. But nothing happened. After a moment, which she, at least, felt was tense, she started to frame an apology. But she'd blurted out only a couple of words when he cut her off with a curt, "It doesn't matter."

She wanted to protest that it *did* matter. She wasn't accustomed to causing her clients even small inconveniences, which was one of the reasons why her limousine service was doing so well in a field that was becoming increasingly competitive.

She resisted further comment on her business practices, then after a minute asked, "Was there anywhere else you wanted to go before we head back to Cape Cod?"

"No," her passenger said shortly.

As she drove past Boston's Chinatown and turned onto the Southeast Expressway, Tory tried to tell herself that there was no such thing as a "thick silence." Silence was silence, no reason to feel that this particular silence was filling her ears with wads of invisible cotton stuffing.

She was startled when, into the silence, Christopher Kendall said suddenly, "I'm sorry. I should have mentioned this before we got on the expressway. Could you turn off somewhere and find a place where I could get a sandwich?"

"A plain place or a fancy place?" Tory asked him.

"Plain will be fine," he said, and retreated into the cotton-wool silence again.

Tory turned off the highway at Braintree, remembering a popular eating spot, and a few minutes later pulled up to the restaurant entrance.

She waited. Nothing happened. She began to wonder if her passenger expected her to come around and open the door for him, though he'd seemed capable enough of doing that for himself back in Boston.

Finally he said irritably, "Why are you stopping here?"

"To let you out," Tory said.

"Here? I don't believe you're supposed to park in front of the entrance."

"I'm not parking. I'll let you out and then find a parking place from which I can see the door. So when you come out—"

"Do you really expect me to leave you in the car?" he asked, venting an annoyance that surprised her. "It's cold out. Damned cold, as a matter of fact."

His voice was a shade icier than the weather as he added, "Find a place to park on the lot, and we'll walk back."

It was a command, and Tory tended to resent commands. But the invitation—if it could be called that—was too good to ignore. Except that as she locked up the Caddy, then started across the parking lot with Christopher Kendall at her side, it dawned on her she was not ready to share a late lunch or anything else with him.

She wasn't dressed for the occasion. She was wearing her working clothes. Her thick, taffy-blond hair was coiled under a chauffeur's cap. Her blue jeans were serviceable, but not fashionable. They were plain old jeans, no designer labels attached. She wore a turtleneck white sweater and a heavy, dark blue wool coat, the general idea being to give the sartorial effect of a uniform that wasn't really a uniform but still connoted...efficiency?

Inside the restaurant foyer she excused herself quickly and headed for the ladies' lounge. Whisking off the chauffeur's cap, she quickly arranged her hair in a makeshift chignon, then daubed on some lipstick and wished she had an eyebrow pencil with her.

Christopher Kendall was waiting for her as she stepped out into the foyer again, and so was the hostess who quickly led them to a booth. Tory slid onto smooth, fake red leather and was almost afraid to so much as glance at her companion. She couldn't remember having felt so ill at ease since her father had taken her to the Ritz-Carlton in Boston to have tea with her Great-Aunt Della, when she was ten years old. Every atom of Great-Aunt Della had been Proper Bostonian. She had squelched children with even the slightest of glances. She didn't even have to speak to make the point that children were intended to be seen, perhaps, but definitely not to be heard . . . ever.

Now Tory suddenly felt that all her fingers had turned into thumbs, and her tongue had become a large thumb, too. So large it could easily block her vocal chords.

She swallowed hard and then coughed. "Are you all right?" Christopher Kendall asked.

Tory looked at him and blinked. He'd taken off the dark glasses, and his eyes were . . . beautiful. Deep dark blue, they reminded her of the sea in winter.

He paraphrased his question. "Is something wrong?" he demanded.

"No," Tory managed quickly and reached for the menu, shaken by the impact his face, in total, was making on her.

A waitress hovered. "What would you like to have?" Christopher Kendall asked politely.

"A club sandwich and tea with lemon, please," Tory said.

"Make it two," he told the waitress.

With the waitress gone, the uncomfortable cotton silence descended again. Tory sought for a way to grope through it, and wished *he'd* take the initiative. Halfway through his sandwich, he finally did.

"Is Tory your real name?" he asked.

"My nickname," she said. "My full name is Victoria."

"Ah," he murmured.

She scowled. She didn't like the sound of that "Ah." "I use my nickname for business purposes," she said. "And it really *is* my nickname."

She knew he'd caught her defensiveness when he mused, "Why do I get the impression you think I'm accusing you of something? Like hiding behind a man's identity, perhaps?"

"I am not . . ." she began hotly.

He actually smiled. Which was enough, in itself, to halt her words in midstream. His smile was like a ray of pure sunshine stabbing through the gloom of a dark afternoon.

"I'm not accusing you of sailing under false pretenses," he said mildly. "There's no reason why a woman shouldn't operate a limousine service. Also, not everyone can offer a beautifully restored '59 Eldorado as a method of conveyance. Where did you get the car?"

"It was one of the last cars my father and I restored together," Tory said before she stopped to think, then wished she'd hedged the question. One revelation could easily lead to another, and she didn't want to talk about herself that much.

"Was that your father's business?" he asked. "Restoring vintage cars?"

"No. It was his hobby. It's my business," Tory said and again cursed her wayward tongue. She could have let it remain a thumb, she told herself. Should have let it block her vocal chords. Nevertheless . . . it was fascinating to see a gleam of interest in her lunch companion's dark blue eyes. "Curiositie," like a shoe that could be passed back and forth, had temporarily slid on to another foot.

"You run a limousine service, and you also restore vintage cars?" he asked. "Doesn't that constitute two full-time jobs?"

She smiled wryly. "Of necessity, the limo business comes first," she confessed. "It pays the routine bills, at least that's its purpose. Restoring antique cars isn't entirely a labor of love—it *is* necessary that I make a profit from it and, of course, each time I make a sale, I do. But obviously one doesn't restore an old car in a day. There's a great deal of time, effort, and what I think of as tender, loving care involved. So I have to make the cars a second priority. . . ."

She paused, surprised at herself for having said so much to him.

"I've never been into cars myself," he said, "but I do know the effort, even the agony, required to produce any good product. To get back to your limo business, though—you must have quite a lot of competition, don't you?"

She nodded. "I've been at it for over a year," she said. "I was a latecomer, and the field—the competition—is still increasing. But there's a lot of need for transportation on the Cape, a growing need, actually."

"Most of your trips are to Boston?"

"Not necessarily," she said. "The longer trips are the most lucrative, of course, but I do a lot of short runs as well. I have one client who hires me an afternoon a week to take her shopping, then to the beauty parlor, then out somewhere to lunch. There are more and more professionals moving to the Cape, too, who commute to their jobs in Boston, and those who can afford it, as a lot of them can, prefer door-to-door limousine service to taking a bus. Then there are people who don't want to risk being caught driving under the influence of alcohol—now that there's such a country-wide campaign against drunk driving—and they'd rather pay to be transported than risk arrest.''

"Are you saying you chauffeur people like that around from bar to bar?''

"No,'' Tory laughed. "It's usually a matter of arranging to pick up someone at a specific place where they've been attending a party, something like that. There are a lot of cabs operating on the Cape, and they get most of the drunks, I'm glad to say.''

"What made you decide to get into the limo business?'' he asked curiously.

"I had to do something if I was going to keep my house in Chatham for long and eat as well,'' Tory said honestly. "A friend who works at a garage in Chatham brought up the idea of my starting a limo service. You don't need a special driver's license, as you do to drive a cab. You can't operate on an 'on call' basis—that's to say you can't go into active competition with taxis. They have their place, you have yours. But,'' Tory finished philosophically, "there's room for all of us.

"The one bummer in running a limo service is the cost of the liability insurance you have to pay,'' she added. "As the number of limo companies have increased, the premiums have skyrocketed.''

"How many people do you employ?''

A while earlier she would have been embarrassed at having to make this admission, but now she was feeling more comfortable with him. "One," she confessed. "Myself."

Admiration mixed with amusement in his eyes. But he didn't tease her. "Getting back to your antique auto restorations—you must have a great deal of mechanical know-how, Tory."

She smiled. "I started working on cars with my father before I even knew the alphabet," she admitted.

The waitress appeared with their check. Snatching it, Christopher Kendall lapsed into silence as he proffered a credit card and waited for his receipt. He was still quiet as they left the restaurant, and Tory, clamping the chauffeur's hat over her hair and trying to keep up with his stride as they walked across the parking lot, was sharply aware of his sudden change of mood.

She glanced at him surreptitiously, wondering what had caused the change. And she wished she had the nerve to come out and ask him directly what was wrong.

Suddenly it occurred to her that maybe he wasn't worrying about himself, but about someone else. Maybe he hadn't gone to the hospital complex to keep an appointment but, rather to visit someone. Someone close to him, who might be very ill.

But if that were the case, wouldn't he have driven himself?

They reached the Caddy. Tory wondered if maybe her passenger might opt for riding in front so they could talk some more. He didn't. He had put the dark glasses on again. He climbed into the back seat, and relapsed into silence. A silence he maintained throughout the balance of the long drive back to the Cape.

It was as if the interlude in the restaurant had never happened.

It was dusk when, her day's work done, Tory bedded the Caddy down in the garage, then let herself into her house through the kitchen door.

She switched on lights, shrugged off her heavy wool coat and tossed the chauffeur's cap on a chair. It was cold in the kitchen, cold enough to make her shiver. This morning, she'd turned the thermostat down in the interest of economy. Now she turned it up—rationalizing that creature comfort had some rights, too—and poured herself a glass of wine.

As she settled in at the kitchen table with her wine, she thought—not for the first time—that she should get herself a dog, or maybe a kitten, for companionship. It was two years since her father had died, and she still missed him very much. Living by oneself was a lonely business.

On the other hand, living alone was better than living with the wrong person. That, she reminded herself, she'd discovered the hard way. She'd tried marriage. It hadn't worked. Her husband had accused her of running home to Daddy, and maybe she had. But she'd found it impossible to stay with a man whom she'd discovered to be dishonest both in his business dealings and in his personal relationships. During the first months after she'd left Randy Baker, she'd often wondered how long he'd been cheating on her with other women before she found him out. The question had never been answered, nor was it ever likely to be. But now, with their divorce long since finalized, it no longer mattered. Randy was part of a past she wouldn't re-live, even if she could.

Her father—ah, that was something else again. They'd shared a very special rapport, for they'd had only each other. Tory remembered reading a novel, when she was about sixteen, in which a man's wife had died in childbirth and he'd hated the child as a result. She'd become so upset that Jeffrey Morgan had finally prodded out of her what was bothering her, and had stared at her aghast.

"Hate you?" he'd echoed, shocked. "My God, Tory, I've always considered you the precious gift your mother left me when she could no longer stay with me herself. How would I have ever managed life without you?"

He would have managed. As she sipped her wine, Tory thought about that and was sure he would have managed. He'd been a strong man. Not perfect. He'd had a stubborn streak in him that she'd inherited, a fierce temper when aroused, and every now and then he would take too much to drink. On those occasions, though, he would merely slip into a mood of quiet introspection, and Tory always had been sure he was thinking about her mother. . . .

The phone rang, its jangle cutting into her memories, and she was glad. She'd already been affected, to-day, by Christopher Kendall's dark mood, she didn't want to conjure up an added cloud of her own.

She was thinking about Christopher Kendall as she walked over to the wall phone and picked up the receiver. So it seemed almost uncanny when she heard his voice at the other end of the line.

"I hope I'm not disturbing you," he said.

"No," Tory said quickly, though he *was* disturbing her. Not in the way he meant—he wasn't interrupting anything—but because he'd made such a deep and mixed impression on her today.

Paramount was the unhappiness she'd sensed about him, the tension, the preoccupation with something that certainly couldn't be pleasant. But there was also the other side of the coin. She'd discovered as they lunched together—though she'd done most of the talking—that he wasn't so self-absorbed it prevented him from being interested and curious about other things and other people. Her limo business, as an example. And she'd also discovered that he was a disturbingly attractive, sexy man with a great deal more to him than surface good looks.

"Tory?"

"Yes?"

"I'd like to set up some dates with you if you have a moment," he said. "Do you have a calendar?"

"A calendar?"

"Yes. I'll be needing transportation to Commonwealth Medical each Wednesday for the next three weeks," he said. "I would have brought that up with you when you let me off this afternoon, but I needed to check my own calendar first. I thought I'd better touch bases before too long, though, to be sure you're not already booked."

"Hold on," Tory said. "Let me get my appointment book."

As she dashed into the living room and took her appointment book out of a desk drawer, Tory was praying that she'd be free on the dates he wanted. She had quite a few Boston trips lined up, and they weren't commitments that could be juggled easily.

She held her breath as he read off dates to her, and was surprised at the extent of her relief when she was able to say, "Those times will all be fine with me."

"Great," he said. "I'll see you next Wednesday, then. My appointment is at ten, so I suppose we should leave here by eight?"

"Seven-thirty," Tory corrected. "That may seem like a lot of leeway, but the morning traffic into Boston can jam up when you least want it to."

"Okay," he agreed, and Tory waited for him to say goodbye. Instead he asked, "Are you presently restoring a car?"

"Yes," she told him. "Right now I'm working on the most exciting car ever to come my way."

"What would that be?"

"A 1930 Pierce-Arrow. Absolutely gorgeous," she enthused, "though it has been sadly neglected. But, fortunately, it was garaged, so although there has been rust to contend with, the actual paint finish is amazingly undamaged. This is a Series 133, a real prize. Eight cylinder..."

"They stopped making Pierce-Arrows a long time ago, didn't they?" he queried.

"In 1937," Tory said promptly. "The company was a relatively small one, located in Buffalo, New York. Their emphasis was on quality...so it's easy to understand why they went out of business after thirty-six years of production. But while they were at it, they made the most distinctive American luxury cars that have ever been produced."

"What color is this one?"

"A very deep blue," Tory began, then stopped abruptly and bit back the rest of her words. She'd been about to say, *Almost exactly the color of your eyes.*

"The car's a roadster," she said, instead. "I'll be replacing the canvas top, also the trunk is covered in canvas and that will have to be redone, too. There's lots of chrome trim, which I'm having replated. Fortunately the traditional Pierce-Arrow symbol on the hood is in remarkably good shape."

"What was the traditional Pierce-Arrow symbol?"

"An Indian holding a bow and arrow."

"What will you do with the car once you've finished restoring it?"

"Sell it," Tory said briefly. "For, I hope, a very, very good price. This car's a rarity."

"You sell all the cars you restore?"

"I have so far, except for the Caddy."

"That must be hard," he said perceptively. "I imagine one could become pretty attached to an antique auto."

"One can," Tory agreed.

"Maybe you'll let me take a look at the Pierce-Arrow, one of these days," he said, to her surprise. Then, before she could comment, added, "I won't keep you any longer. See you next Wednesday."

Tory stared at the phone receiver for a long moment before she set it down gently. A whole series of questions began whirling through her head again.

"Curiositie," that age-old, dangerous commodity, was reaching the brimming-over point.

Chapter Two

Tory pulled up in front of Christopher Kendall's house at twenty-five minutes past seven Wednesday morning. He didn't keep her waiting. He quickly came down the front steps, once again wearing the perfectly tailored cashmere coat and the dark glasses.

He crossed to the car, and before Tory was aware of what he was going to do, he opened the front door and slid onto the bucket seat next to hers.

"Good morning," he said.

"Good morning," she answered, trying to maintain a pleasant but professional attitude.

During the past week, she'd been unable to resist testing out her personal grapevine in town. She'd put forth some questions about Christopher Kendall; some answers had come back to her, making her almost wish she hadn't asked the questions in the first place.

He was even wealthier, even more socially promi-
nent than she'd thought him to be. In short, he was not
the kind of man with whom she should tangle. Not that
he'd tried to tangle with her the other day. His tack had
been very much the opposite, initially. But, for a while
in the restaurant, and later when he'd called her to book
the chauffeuring dates, she'd felt a certain climate
change between them. A heightened awareness, interest and sexual chemistry, had begun to combine in a
brew that wasn't all that potent yet, but had the capa-
bility of becoming so.

Tory also had sensed the possibility that maybe the
two of them shared at least one common problem, a
problem that could be even more dangerous than that
chemistry.

Maybe for all his wealth and prestige, Christopher
Kendall was as lonely as she was. And, as she knew well,
there was a vulnerability to being lonely that sometimes prompted a reaching out, which could later be
regretted. It wouldn't help either of them for that to
happen.

As she started the Caddy, Tory saw that Christopher
was gazing through the windshield, scanning the sky.
"The weather forecast sounded pretty miserable," he
said. "We might even run into some snow."

"If it does snow, the snow won't lay," Tory predicted. "Snow never does last, this time of year."

He grinned. "Seems to me I've heard of some pretty
heavy blizzards occurring in March."

"Unusual," she said.

"Let's hope you're right."

They fell silent for a time, and the silence was surprisingly companionable today. But he didn't let it last.
"How's the Pierce-Arrow?" he asked.

"Just about where she was the last time I saw you," Tory admitted. "I haven't been able to put in much time on her. This will be my third trip to Boston so far this week, and it's only Wednesday. But I'm not complaining."

"I take it you've built up a list of repeat customers?"

"I'm building up a list of repeat customers," she corrected. "As I'm sure you know, we have a lot of retired people living year-round on the Cape these days, and a majority of them like to travel. So there's considerable business back and forth to Logan Airport. I took a couple up to Logan Monday, then yesterday I drove up to meet another couple who were just returning from a Caribbean cruise."

"You must book well ahead."

"I do."

"Then I was lucky you were free on my dates."

Tory didn't comment on that, and after a moment he switched the subject. "Did you go to business college?" he asked, to her surprise.

"No," she said. "What makes you think I might have?"

"Because in this age we're living in it takes more than native know-how to run a business successfully," he said.

She smiled, "Mine is not really that big a business, Mr. Kendall."

"Chris?" he suggested.

"Chris."

"Even to run a small business takes expertise," he persisted.

"Not in comparison to a business like yours," Tory said without stopping to think, a bad habit she sometimes fell into.

His, "Oh?" sounded as chilly as the weather outside. Tory took her eyes off the road just long enough to glance sideways at him. She was not surprised to see an eloquent eyebrow arched over the rim of his dark glasses. "Chatham's a small town," she said hastily. "People know who you are. You must be aware of that."

"I suppose so," he admitted. "But it's a long time since I've been around Chatham. The house has been closed much of that time. It was a spur-of-the-moment decision on my part to reopen it in the dead of winter. But I wanted somewhere I could be by myself...."

"To recoup from your accident?" Again Tory let her words escape too quickly.

She saw him take off the dark glasses, was aware of a blue blaze searing through the distance between them. And there was a caustic note in his voice as he commented, "You *have* been doing your homework, haven't you?"

Tory flushed. She resented his tone of voice—the obvious censure made her feel as if she was being convicted without the benefit of a trial. On the other hand . . . he had a right to be annoyed. No one liked the thought of having questions asked behind their back.

Chris put the dark glasses back on again. Then, his tone milder, he said, "Would you mind telling me what your informant—or informants—had to say about me? I think I should have the right to give you my own version of anything I don't agree with."

"Please," Tory protested, wishing she could come upon a rest area so she could pull the car off the road and talk to him about this without having to concentrate on the morning rush-hour traffic as well. "No one said anything detrimental."

"Well," he observed wryly, "that's nice to hear."

"Chris, please. I'm sorry. What I mean to say is that I—well, I happened to run into someone in town, and your name came up."

That was the truth, but not the whole truth. She'd had business at the garage where Hank Chase worked. He was one of the best mechanics she'd ever met. She had total faith in him, and he often pitched in when she needed help on a car restoration.

The particular matter she'd wanted to discuss with him could, however, have waited awhile longer. She'd sought Hank out because she knew he'd lived in Chatham most of his life, and she quickly discovered she'd come to the right person. Hank had volunteered that he'd known Chris Kendall since they both were kids, though he hadn't seen much of him in recent years. Chris had been a "summer person," back in those days, but they were the same age—now thirty-six—and they'd both participated in some of the town's summertime activities.

With a chuckle, Hank had recalled the time he and Chris had competed in a Fourth of July swimming race. Chris had been the first one to reach the floating watermelon, which had been the big prize of the day.

Hank also had volunteered that Chris was still a bachelor, as far as he knew, but he'd evidently had a string of involvements with women if one were to believe what they read in gossip columns.

"Well?" Chris asked, jolting Tory back from some errant speculations.

She clutched the wheel a little tighter. While Hank had talked openly about Chris and hadn't asked her to keep what he said in confidence, she still hated repeating things people told her. Nevertheless, she owed Chris an explanation.

"I understand," she said, struggling with the words, "that your family has roots on Cape Cod that go a long way back, even though no one in your immediate branch has made the Cape a full-time home for a long time."

"That's true enough."

"Well . . . I also understand you're the last of your particular line."

That, she was tempted to add, gave them something in common. He was evidently the last of his branch of the Kendalls. She was the last of her branch of the Morgans.

"Go on," he invited.

"Your family business, Kendall Boats, started here on the Cape and later moved onto the mainland near Plymouth. Then over the years the business expanded, and there are now Kendall boatyards in other locations."

As she spoke, Tory was aware that she was not speaking of a run-of-the-mill family business. Kendall Boats, Inc. was a very big business, having long since diversified into a number of areas.

"True," Chris said noncommittally, prompting her to continue.

"Your father died seven years ago," she said, "at which point you became head of the corporation and . . . well, I would gather that the business has flourished, increasingly, ever since."

There was no sound from her passenger.

"You," she went on, feeling that this was getting worse and worse but knowing that there was no way he was going to let her stop, "perfected the plan for the famous Kendall Ketch. The initial design was made by your grandfather, but that was back in an era when the company was so new the management didn't dare risk capital on a boat whose design had not already been tried and proven."

There was still no sound.

"After the launching of your version of the ketch," Tory continued, close to the edge of desperation because his silence was proving to be totally unnerving, "you were widely heralded in boating circles, and your fame as both a designer and builder of boats was assured...."

"Mmm," Chris said.

Tory wasn't about to tell him that Hank had also commented that Chris Kendall was simply a natural at achieving anything he set out to do. He'd always been able to beat anyone around playing tennis. He was an expert water-skier and sailboarder. And he had few rivals when it came to sailing. He'd participated, in fact, in most of the major sailing races, including the America's Cup.

"His luck kind of ran out last fall, though," Hank had said, at this point. "He had an accident while he was on an inspection tour of one of his boatyards."

"What happened?" Tory asked quickly.

"I'm not sure, exactly," Hank admitted. "But whatever it was must have been pretty serious. I heard he was laid up for quite a while and he's down here to convalesce."

Remembering this part of her conversation, Tory darted another quick glance at her passenger. He looked like anything but a convalescent.

When she didn't continue, Chris demanded, "Well?"

"I think that's enough, don't you?"

"That depends," he said. "Tory?"

"Yes?"

"Who told you all this stuff about me?"

Tory had a strong conviction that if she didn't volunteer the information to Chris he'd persist until he found out for himself who her informant had been.

"I was talking with Hank Chase down at Melson's Garage," she said, feeling miserable. "He said he used to know you."

"*Used* to know me?" Chris echoed. "Is *that* the way people around town feel? That they used to know me? I didn't realize I'd gotten so out of step."

"Hank was remembering summers, years past, that was all," Tory said quickly. "Times, I guess, when you were around more than you've been in recent years."

"I've been a hell of a lot busier in recent years," he pointed out to her. "Also, the Cape's not usually on my beaten path. Kendall's main boatyard is in Essex, Connecticut, these days. We maintain the South Shore boatyard near Plymouth, as well, but our second largest boatyard, now, is in Florida, on the Gulf Coast. Last year we also opened a boatyard in California. And then Kendall, Inc., is into a few other enterprises. Anyway..."

Tory filled in the silence, this time. "Do you live in Connecticut?" she asked him.

"No, I live in New York. The executive offices are in Manhattan, and that's where I work, primarily, except for inspection tours and necessary troubleshooting when no one else seems able to solve a problem. I maintain a condo in Manhattan. I also have a condo in Florida, and a beach place near San Diego. Anything else?''

Tory could feel the heat seeping into her cheeks. But she felt she had a right to the resentment that was surging. "I wasn't trying to pry," she said hotly. Then, because honesty was such a basic part of her nature—she'd been told more than once she was too honest for her own good—she added, "I admit I felt a . . . a natural curiosity about you. But I can assure you from now on I'll mind my own business."

Chris Kendall chuckled. "I'm not sure *I* will," he said. "Tory . . . don't look so stricken. If you were curious enough about me to bring up my name to Hank Chase, I'm flattered. Anyway . . ."

"Yes?"

"Maybe it would help if you knew I'm equally curious about you, Victoria Morgan. To the point where I've been doing my homework, too."

"What are you saying?"

"It happens," Chris observed laconically, "that I needed a haircut a couple of days ago and so sought the services of Howie Nickerson. You know Howie?"

"Yes, I know Howie."

"It wasn't busy in the barbershop that morning, so Howie and I had time to chat a little. I asked him if he knew you, and he said he did and for years he used to cut your father's hair, summers."

"That's so."

"Well, Howie wasn't about to tell any tales out of school," Chris said, a mischievous smile playing about his lips as he spoke. "But he did volunteer that you were divorced a while back and came home to Chatham where your father was recuperating from a heart attack. Howie said that since your father's death two years ago, you've been living here alone, year-round, restoring cars and running your limo service. I'd say from Howie's enthusiasm the locals think pretty highly of you, and their respect is not easily achieved.''

Tory was so staggered she couldn't answer him. And, for once, she was glad the traffic was heavy for she had more motivation than ever to concentrate on her driving.

Chris was willing to lapse into silence again. He'd already said more than he'd intended to say. Certainly he hadn't intended to mention his question-and-answer session with Howie Nickerson. But he'd suddenly felt that Tory Morgan had the right to know her curiosity about him had been matched by his curiosity about her.

As they neared Boston, he slumped back and closed his eyes wearily, fighting the urge to press his temples and try to push away the headache that was taking throbbing possession of him again. But he felt sure the gesture would be much too telltale, only leading to further curiosity on Tory's part. And he wasn't about to get into his medical problems with anyone.

Last week, when he'd gone up to Commonwealth Complex to consult with the surgeon who'd operated on him in November, he had hoped to take away with him a prescription for medication that would take care of the headache pain until the headaches themselves finally ceased.

As he'd feared might be the case, the problem hadn't been that simple. Chris had felt obligated to admit that he was still having occasional blackouts. They never lasted long, he'd protested, when the surgeon had looked a shade too grave upon hearing that. And, when his vision returned, after one of the episodes he could see as clearly as ever.

Even as he'd made his admission, Chris realized he was talking about a condition that was one of the major reasons why he'd needed surgery in the first place. The surgery was supposed to have corrected the blackouts. He had assumed that maybe the correction took a while, that the blackouts would come less and less frequently and finally phase out altogether. But a look at the surgeon's face warned him he was wrong.

There was to be no instant diagnosis, he soon discovered. No instant prognosis. A series of tests were in order, spaced a week apart. With that information in hand, Chris had left the hospital, thoroughly frustrated.

Now, approaching the Commonwealth Complex again, the frustration returned in full force. He'd already been away from the helm of his business for nearly five months. Though he kept in constant touch by phone with headquarters in New York, as well as with his boatyards and offices in other sections of the country, absentee leadership left much to be desired.

He needed to get back to work. He'd worked most of his life, though he imagined most people would find that hard to believe. And he was used to taking charge of whatever he did. Since taking over as company head after his father's death, there were many times when he'd wished he could delegate even more management authority than he did, but he'd learned early on that to run a company successfully the top man had to be present and accounted for. Nevertheless, his true love was designing. His biggest satisfaction in life to date had come from his perfection of his grandfather's design for the Kendall Ketch. There were designs for other boats mulling around in his head, and under other circumstances this hiatus in Chatham would have provided the perfect chance to put them down on paper. As it was, the recurring headaches had pretty much prohibited that.

He scowled, and Tory glanced at him again just in time to see the scowl. She realized it wasn't directed at her and wondered what it *was* directed at.

She didn't have time to think about much of anything for a while after that, except the rush hour traffic piling into Boston. In a couple of important areas there was road repair work in progress, which added to the confusion.

"It's lucky we left on the early side," Tory told Chris, once they had pulled off the Southeast Expressway and were inching through Boston's narrow, cluttered, downtown streets.

It was only a few minutes before ten when she drove up in front of the Commonwealth Medical Complex. "I'll probably be three hours," Chris said tersely. "Maybe a little more, maybe a little less. Why don't you roam around and park in the hospital lot when you come back? I'll wait for you in the lobby or you can wait for me, whichever way it turns out."

With that he was gone, striding toward the entrance with long steps that had a communicable urgency about them.

Tory had sensed the change in him, the closer they got to the city, and now she was tempted to run after him. She wanted to say, "Good luck," wanted to say something to him, anyhow, though she had absolutely no idea of what he was facing.

Again she parked near the Copley Place shopping area and started wandering through the stores. She'd deliberately left her checkbook at home, and she had very little cash with her, so this was merely a variety of window-shopping in which she was indulging. Still, it was fun to look, and again she promised herself that soon—maybe after she'd sold the Pierce-Arrow—she'd permit herself the luxury of a few purchases.

She'd never been a big spender, but once in a while she did love splurging on something frivolous, or beautiful, or maybe merely whimsical such as some out-of-season fruit, or a tiny vial of French perfume.

After a time she tired of make-believe shopping, but she wasn't hungry enough to stop for lunch. She asked herself if she was subconsciously waiting for another lunch invitation from Chris Kendall? Maybe, she conceded as she redeemed the car and drove back to the medical complex.

When she went into the hospital lobby, Chris wasn't there. Tory settled down in an armchair, and pulled a slender volume out of her handbag. This time her choice of poets was John Dryden, and soon she was reading the words he'd written back in the seventeenth century that held such appeal for her today.

She became so immersed in her reading that Chris was standing right next to her before she was aware of his presence.

Startled, she dropped the book. Chris reached down, picked it up and surveyed the title. Then he sat down in the armchair next to hers, and observed, "Not exactly escape reading, I'd say."

"I'm something of a fanatic about sixteenth and seventeenth century poets," Tory confessed. "Partly because they said so many things, way back then, that we tend to think of as contemporary."

"Such as?" he challenged.

"Well, John Heywood, back in the 1500s, observed, 'Two heads are better than one,'" Tory reported. "He also said, 'When the iron is hot, strike.' And, 'Look 'ere ye leape,' as well as a lot of other sayings one would think were much more modern."

She was scanning Chris's face as she spoke, trying not to be obvious about it. But she couldn't suppress the pang of concern she felt for him. He looked weary, haggard, pale. She wondered what the doctors had been doing to him over the past three hours.

"What about Dryden?"

"Well," she said, "listen to this."

She picked a verse at random and wished, once she was into it, that she'd scanned the page more carefully. It was too late to back out, though, so she read,

"Our souls sit close and silently within,
And their own web from their own entrails spin;
And when eyes meet far off, our sense is such
That, spider-like, we feel the tenderest touch...."

She had a soft, lovely voice, and a flair for reading poetry. Chris stared at her as the last word shimmered between them, and he thought he'd never seen anyone lovelier. With the chauffeur's cap cast aside, her taffy-colored hair gleamed in the glow cast by the overhead lights. Her eyes were clear gray, fringed by unexpectedly dark lashes. Her skin was slightly flushed—he had the impression that what she'd just read to him had embarrassed her—and he knew that he was going to have to get a copy of Dryden's works and read those lines for himself. There'd been an intimacy about the words. An intimacy about her rendition of them . . .

Chris had been infatuated with many women, but early on, he'd had the sense to realize that there was a wide gap between infatuation and love. Like any wealthy bachelor, he was accustomed to having a proportion of the unattached women he met make a pitch not only for him, but for his money.

His mother had died when he was young, and a year or so later his father had married a woman fifteen years younger than he was. She'd taken the old man for quite a ride, Chris remembered bitterly. The divorce settlement had cost a small fortune. But it was the job this experience had done on his father's morale, rather than the exorbitant amount of cash involved, that had stuck with Chris. In his opinion, his father had gone downhill ever since the day his second wife walked out on him. The blow to his pride was enormous, and Lionel Kendall was a man with a great deal of pride. Chris had inherited that same kind of pride, and after his father's divorce he had made up his mind that no woman alive was ever going to do a similar thing to him.

No woman had. And his resolution that no woman would was as strong as ever. But his father's experience had caused him to view women with an edge of suspicion that, so far, had let him go just so far but no farther in his relationships.

Tory Morgan was an entirely different kind of woman than he'd ever met before, he realized that. But those same negative suspicions had surfaced today when he'd found out Tory had been asking questions about him around town.

Then, watching her stammer out what she'd learned, he'd suddenly realized that actually Tory had been curious about him in the same way he was about her. She was interested in him. Not in his money. In him.

Looking at her now, he realized that an involvement with someone like Tory Morgan might very well lead past infatuation to love. Not that he was about to have any sort of personal involvement with her, Chris added to himself hastily, even though he couldn't recall ever seeing a woman who looked more desirable than Tory did right now.

This was not the moment for such errant thoughts. He had enough on his mind, Chris reminded himself. The last thing he needed was a woman who might affect him to a far greater extent than he wanted to be affected.

He stood as Tory put the slender poetry volume back into her handbag, and said tersely, "Let's get out of here, shall we?"

He was on his feet before she could answer him, and at the hospital entrance before she could catch up with him. There she said breathlessly, "If you'll just wait here, I'll go get the car out of the lot and bring it around."

"I'm capable of walking, thank you," Chris snapped. "I'll come with you. And for God's sake, don't cram that chauffeur's cap back down on your head. It makes you look like you're trying out for a 1920's vaudeville act."

Chris was heading toward the hospital parking lot as he spoke. Tory stood still and let him go. She didn't know why he'd just exploded, but she'd recognized his need to let off steam. Maybe it had to do with her, but not entirely, she thought. She was certain that Chris was going through a real ordeal and keeping everything connected with it bottled up inside him. She knew the feeling. She, too, had no one with whom to share her crises.

Chris reached the top of a flight of stone steps that led down to the parking lot, then turned. His voice carried across the space between them.

"Coming?" he asked.

Tory moved toward him slowly, and was abreast of him when he reached out to clasp her arm. She would have sworn that his hand felt warm, even through the thick fabric of her dark blue coat. Then, with his other hand, he gently touched her cheek, rubbing her skin ever so softly in a small circular movement.

His touch was electric, telegraphing messages Tory was sure Chris wouldn't even have considered verbalizing just now. And she felt herself possessed of the power to read and interpret the signals he was sending her while his fingers continued to barely feather-touch her cheek. He was communicating that he was weary and hurting and frustrated and alone. His touch told her all those things.

Tory wished she had the courage to reach up and whip off the dark glasses, to stare deeply into his incredible blue eyes and try to figure it all out. She wished even more that she had the courage to ask him to explain it to her.

She felt a sudden flow of emotion wash over her like a warm wave, bringing with it a riptide of bittersweet stirrings. Looking up, she met the opaque lenses of Chris's dark glasses. "We'd better get back to the car," he said rather unsteadily, though he was still clutching her arm.

Side by side, they walked down the stone steps.

Chapter Three

Snow materialized a few miles south of Boston. Heavy wet snow that plopped down on the windshield and the hood.

"Rats," Tory muttered as she started the windshield wipers arcing back and forth.

Chris, who had appeared to be lost in a reverie, roused himself. "Want me to drive?" he asked.

Tory was dumbfounded. "No," she retorted. Then added, "You can't, anyway."

"Of course I can," he snapped. "Hell, I was driving surreptitiously by the time I was thirteen years old. Even before then, when I could just about see over the steering wheel, I used to sneak my father's four-wheel-drive and take it down on the dunes."

"Didn't you ever get caught?"

"Yeah, eventually I got caught. The cop didn't press charges, but my father restricted me to the premises. No 'privileges' for longer than I like to think about."

"I don't understand this," Tory said after a pause. "If you can drive, why do you hire a limo service?"

"It's a long story," Chris said. He added bluntly, "And I have no intention of getting into it. I only wanted you to know that if driving in the snow bothers you, I'll be glad to take over."

He lapsed back into silence, wishing he could retract what he'd just said or at least the way in which he'd said it. Tory didn't deserve that kind of curtness.

Sneaking a glance at her face, he saw that it was as expressionless as she could make it, a clue that he'd hurt her feelings with his abruptness. As he watched, she frowned, and he suspected she was trying to rationalize his behavior, trying to figure him out. That was understandable. Were their roles reversed, he was sure he'd be doing the same thing.

As it was, his offer to drive had been made on impulse because he thought she looked tired and seemed a little bit overwrought. The offer had been a safe enough one. His ebony curtain descended slowly when it descended; he'd have plenty of warning so he could get off the highway and turn the controls back over to Tory. That's what he'd been thinking when he made the suggestion to her, which he could see in retrospect had been a very stupid suggestion to make. Tory was a professional driver. He couldn't blame her if she'd taken his offer as an aspersion cast on her competency.

As if verifying this, she asked suddenly, "Do you *want* to drive?"

"No," he said.

"I mean, you haven't developed doubts about my abilities, have you?"

"Of course not. You're one of the best drivers I've ever been in a car with. I only wanted to help you out if I could." As he spoke, Chris was beginning to feel that he owed Tory an explanation about quite a few things, most especially his erratic behavior. He began impulsively, "Tory—" And then came to a sudden stop. It was hitting him that though he was great at dealing with people in business-related matters, the same didn't apply on a personal level. He was too conditioned to keeping his personal feelings, his personal problems, strictly to himself.

"Tory..." he began again.

"Yes?"

"I know I'm not the easiest person in the world to be around," he admitted. "But...bear with me, will you? I'm—well, I'm going through a difficult time."

"Do you want to talk about it?"

"No," he said honestly, again wishing he could retract what he'd just told her. No woman in the world would let him off the hook after a revelation such as that.

Tory surprised him. "All right," she said, then added with a touch of impishness, "And, just for the record, I'll bear with you. Okay?"

By the time they reached the bridge over the Cape Cod Canal, the snow was turning to fast-falling sleet. The driving became all the more hazardous. Very conscious of Chris at her side, Tory handled the car as if she were driving on eggshells.

As she pulled up in front of his house, she suddenly wished he'd ask her to come in. For a cup of coffee, maybe, or just to get warm in front of the fire his servants undoubtedly would have blazing on the hearth. She wanted to be with him a little longer. She had the feeling that if they could extend this time today, he might reach the point of telling her about the invisible burden he was carrying.

But Chris said only "See you next week. Take care, meantime." And she watched him trudge alone through the mushy combination of snow and sleet toward his front door.

The weather was still miserable on Thursday, and the client scheduled for a trip to Providence canceled. Tory was glad of the chance to stay home. She did a few things around the house that needed doing, then spent some highly satisfactory hours in her underground garage. Working with her hands always had a calming effect on her. Handling the tools her father had passed on to her was a kind of therapy, and the concentration required in this kind of work taught mental discipline, thus how to block out thoughts and problems that could be better dealt with another day.

Each of her tools had its place, and one of the first rules her father had taught her was that every tool should be put away in that place before calling a halt. Once the garage was in order, Tory gave the Pierce-Arrow one last, loving look. The car's restoration was coming along beautifully. Before long, she was going to have to think of finding the right buyer...and that was going to be hard. It was always difficult to part with a car once she'd restored it. She grew to love them all. But the Pierce was so very special.

Back upstairs, Tory settled for canned chicken noodle soup for her dinner, watched TV for a while, then indulged in a hot bubble bath before heading for bed.

At this point she was tired physically, which was good. Being tired physically usually carried with it the promise of a good night's sleep. Being mentally or emotionally tired usually indicated just the opposite. Her problem was that tonight she was tired in all three ways, so it depended upon whether the physical, mental, or emotional fatigue would dominate.

Whichever... she couldn't get Chris Kendall out of her mind.

The next four days passed slowly. Then, the weekend over, Monday edged into Tuesday and Tuesday into Wednesday when, once again, Tory presented herself at Chris's house at seven-twenty in the morning.

It was a bright sunny day. There was even a hint of spring in the air. Chris looked fit and well rested and seemed in a good frame of mind. He smiled across at her as he slid into the bucket seat by her side, and it took an effort on her part to return the smile in the same lighthearted way with which it had been given.

Tory had talked to herself all week about this man now sitting beside her, and she was determined to keep things on a casual basis between them today. If he'd wanted to indulge in any confidences with her, Chris would have called her during the week, she told herself for perhaps the twentieth time. Certainly she'd been available. She'd spent most of her time dividing her attention between the Pierce and a '51 Chrysler Saratoga Club Coupé she was restoring, and there was a phone extension in the underground garage.

Chris hadn't called, though, and as each day passed Tory had talked to herself a little louder. She'd hit this man at a vulnerable time, or he wouldn't have even confided as much in her as he had. But, primarily, he'd hired her to chauffeur him back and forth to Boston.

That's what he wanted from her, no more, no less. Today was the second of the three extra dates he'd booked with her. Next Wednesday would be their last Wednesday. She wasn't sure how she'd handle it if he needed further chauffeuring.

Chris Kendall not only had been haunting her daytime hours this past week, but he'd been slipping into her dreams. In those dreams, their relationship acquired quite a different dimension. Last night, he'd made love to her.…

She hastily turned the key in the ignition switch as Chris asked agreeably, "Been keeping busy?"

"Very," she said, which was true.

It was only civil to return the question, so she asked Chris, "What about you?"

"If I sound hoarse, it's because I've spent most of the past few days on the phone," he said, frowning. "I've been away from business too long," he muttered. "I need to get back."

"Problems?" she asked.

"Series of problems," he told her. "Some of legitimate importance, some important only to the individuals dealing with them. Then," he added, "they've been having some incidents of suspected sabotage at the Essex boatyard. It's becoming one of those situations where you're pretty damned sure you know who the guilty party is. But, of course, you have to prove it."

"Who do you think the guilty party is?"

"A disgruntled employee who was fired last fall after…"

Tory waited, and finally asked, "After what?"

"After an incident in the shipyard," Chris said carefully. "This man was responsible for an accident that resulted from his own carelessness. Carelessness largely caused by the fact he'd just come back from lunch, where he'd had a couple of hefty drinks. I used to work in the Essex yard summers, when I was going to college. Anyone working around a shipyard needs all his wits about him. There are too many opportunities for accidents. As a result of this one, there was an in-company investigation that resulted in the unanimous opinion the man should be dismissed...."

"And?"

"We thought he'd left the area," Chris said. "Now it appears he hasn't. He's been seen around Essex recently. No one's sure whether he's been around ever since last fall—maybe hiding out somewhere in the vicinity—or whether he loomed up again recently. Regardless, there have been a couple of odd happenings at the boatyard. Nothing too serious, yet. But there was a minor fire recently that seems to have been of suspicious origin. My men in charge down in Essex point to this character as a logical saboteur or arsonist, and they're afraid he's merely been toying around so far, possibly paving the way for something a lot bigger. I have to admit they may be right."

Chris slumped down in the seat, leaned his head back against the upholstery. "I didn't mean to get into such a dissertation," he said.

Tory ignored his last comment. "Does this man have a personal vendetta against anyone in your company, Chris?" she asked.

Chris hesitated for a moment, then said exactly what she'd been afraid he was going to say. "Yes," he told her. "Me."

When they reached the hospital, Chris once again told Tory he wasn't sure exactly how long he'd be.

Probably about three hours, he estimated. And, as he had before, he suggested she roam around for a while then meet him in the lobby.

Tory cut short her store browsing, anxious not to keep Chris waiting if he finished early. But when she reached the hospital lobby, he was not in sight.

She settled down in an armchair and, once again, drew a small, leather-bound volume out of her handbag. This one contained some of the works of Christopher Marlowe, another of her sixteenth-century favorites.

She tried to immerse herself in the poet's lyrical words, but failed. Her mind was too filled with conjecture and worry about Chris.

This time she saw him immediately as he emerged from an elevator, looked around, spotted her and then strode toward her.

Watching him approach, she became aware, anew, of how tall and perfectly proportioned he was. And, of how he moved with the grace of a natural athlete. Yes, she could imagine that all the things Hank Chase had said about Chris's athletic prowess were only too true.

She smiled ruefully. When it came to outdoor achievements, she sometimes felt as if she'd been born with two left feet.

Chris came up to her, observed the book she was holding and asked, "Who are you honoring this time?"

"Christopher Marlowe," Tory said, and automatically held the book out to him.

He took the little volume from her, whipped off his dark glasses and glanced at the page his finger touched. Slowly he read, "'Come live with me and be my love; And we will all the pleasures prove....'"

The words spun out, silken, shimmering. There was a caressing quality to Chris's voice as he read them, and Tory stared up at him, transfixed. Then his eyes met her eyes and held, and she felt as if all the breath were being siphoned out of her. Was it possible for two spirits to touch in the middle of a hospital lobby painted a rather muddy shade of tan, the furniture dark, the atmosphere more dark than light?

Come live with me and be my love . . .

Ask me, Tory thought incoherently. Just ask me.

Tory stood abruptly, staggered by the direction in which her emotions were leading. Chris put his glasses on again, and handed the book back to her. "Quite beautiful," he commented, and Tory couldn't bring herself to answer him.

The traffic was relatively light getting out of Boston. Chris had been intending to ask Tory to have lunch with him on the way back to the Cape, but his head started pounding fiercely before they'd gone very far, and the thought of food became abhorrent.

The pain grew more and more intense. Ironically he was carrying a prescription in his wallet the doctors had just given him. It was for some new medication, which they felt might alleviate the headache pain, which was about the best they could do for him at the moment.

He'd been intending to ask Tory to stop at a pharmacy in Chatham so he could get the prescription filled. But right now Chatham might as well have been a thousand miles away. He knew that long before he could hope to get the medication, he already would have gone through the tortures of the damned.

They were nearly at Plymouth when he managed, "I'm sorry, Tory. I know I've been rotten company, but

I have a . . . hell of a headache. I wanted to ask you to have lunch with me somewhere, but I'm afraid right now . . ."

He heard the anxiety in Tory's voice. "Chris, is there anything I can do?"

He nearly shook his head, but repressed that bit of action just in time. "No," he said thickly. "I have a prescription for some stuff. Once we get to Chatham, I'd appreciate it if you'd go into a pharmacy for me and get it filled. Until then, if I just stay as still as I can . . ."

Looking across at him, Tory saw that his features were rigid, and he was shades paler than usual. She fought the impulse to press her foot down on the accelerator and to rush them back to Devon as fast as the wheels would carry them. This was no time to risk an accident.

But it seemed forever before they finally reached Chatham and she pulled up in front of a pharmacy. Then it seemed forever before the pharmacist finished filling the prescription.

Tory rushed out to the car with the medication and was handing the small package to Chris when she realized he was going to need a glass of water with which to swallow the pills.

She started to tell him so but he interrupted her, an odd note in his voice as he said, "Don't bother. Not now. I can wait till I get home. Just let's *get* home, okay, Tory?"

Tory cast a worried glance at him as she got into the car. He was sitting bolt upright, staring straight ahead. She saw the muscles in his cheek twitch, saw that his lips were pressed together so tightly there was a thin white line etched around them. And she knew that there was something very, very wrong.

* * *

Chris realized there was going to be no way out of telling Tory what was happening, much as he disliked doing so. The curtain had started to descend just about the time she was going into the pharmacy. Now it was more than halfway down, and he knew there was no way of reversing the procedure. No way he could yank the curtain up again. In a short while, he was going to be totally blind.

By the time they left the main road to start up the hillside lane to his house, Chris's personal sun was totally extinguished. He felt the car come to a stop, heard the engine die, presumed Tory had turned off the ignition switch and knew she must be waiting for him to make a move.

Nothing had ever been harder for Chris than to say what he had to say to her. He moistened his lips, started to speak, then had to moisten his lips anew and start all over again.

"Tory," he said carefully, "I hate to tell you this, but I'm afraid I'm going to need your help. You see . . . just now I can't see anything."

He heard her convulsive gasp, her incredulous, *"What?"*

"It's only a temporary condition," Chris said quickly. It comes over me now and then . . . which is the reason why I'm not driving myself around these days. It doesn't happen frequently, but I never know just when it will, and . . ."

Chris felt his arm being grasped by Tory's warm hands. The stiffness of her fingers communicated her tension, but she only said, in a remarkably calm voice, "Okay, how do we handle this?"

Chris actually managed a short laugh. "I suppose we could begin by your taking my arm and helping me up my front walk." He fumbled in his coat pocket and found the key to the front door. "Here," he said, handing it to her. "Suppose we take it that far, and then we'll go into installment two."

Brave words, he soon discovered, because what he'd proposed was easier said than done. Once out of the car, he felt totally disoriented; his sense of direction vanished. "I think it would be easier if you take hold of my arm and sort of follow my lead," Tory said gently. "Your front walk looks pretty level. I don't think there's anything you could trip on."

They started out, Tory moving very slowly. Holding her arm, Chris could feel the tautness of her muscles, and could appreciate how she must be feeling, playing this weird version of blindman's buff. She was being so terribly careful to keep him on course, and not to misstep herself. Moved by this concern for him and his safety, his pressure on her arm increased until Tory stopped suddenly, and asked, "Are you all right?"

"I'm fine," Chris said huskily, fighting back the impulse to grope not just for her arm but for *her*. Suddenly he wanted to pull her close to him, to drown himself in her sweetness....

They began to move forward again. "Okay. We're getting near the steps," Tory said, after a time. "Reach out your foot, Chris, and prod the first step. Feel it?"

"Yes, ma'am," he replied obediently, trying to pretend this whole episode was a joke of sorts.

"Now," she said, "there are five steps up to the top of the stoop. Okay? Hang on a minute, will you, while I open the door?"

She withdrew her arm and, bereft of it, Chris felt as if he'd been set out in alien space. Then Tory reached for his hand again and drew him through his own doorway and through what he knew must be the foyer but—with no visible guidelines—could as well have been someplace on Mars.

Tory expected that someone would loom up in Chris's foyer—a butler, perhaps, or a housemaid—but no one did. She stood, still clutching Chris's hand, and wondered what to do next. Where was the household help? Was this everyone's day off?

She led Chris into a drawing room, which was beautifully furnished, mostly with antiques, which she felt sure must be priceless. "There's a chair just behind you," she said finally. "Go ahead, sit down. I'll get a glass of water so you can take some medication."

Chris sank cautiously into a damask-covered armchair, and after an anxious glance at him Tory started out on a safari to find the kitchen.

On her way, she passed by a library whose bookshelves were lined with jewel-toned volumes. Next she went through a formal dining room, where lovely old silver gleamed on a massive sideboard. Finally she came to the kitchen, which—in contrast to the other rooms—was strictly modern, the only exception to modernity being a big, round pine table, flanked by four wooden chairs.

Tory found a glass, filled it with water and hurried back to Chris with it. She read the instructions on the pill vial aloud, gave him the two tablets prescribed and waited while he swallowed them. Only then did she ask, "Exactly what happens, Chris ... when this happens?"

He said slowly, "It's like having a curtain go down. A sort of filmy black curtain that shuts out your sight. Then after a while, the curtain goes up again and . . . everything's fine."

"How long a while?" she asked.

"Not very long," he hedged.

"Look," she decided, "I'm going back to the kitchen to brew up a pot of coffee. I'll fix some sandwiches, too, if I can find the makings."

"There should be bread and stuff in the fridge," he told her.

"Is this the help's day off?"

Chris frowned. This was the first time he'd been with anyone when he was having one of these spells, and it was disconcerting not to be able to focus on a face when answering a question. He tried to look toward where he thought Tory's face would be, but he didn't know if he was zeroing in on her or missing her entirely. "What help?" he asked her.

"Chris, I assumed you'd have a staff of servants. . . ."

"I don't need a staff of servants," Chris said rather testily. "I'm here by myself, Tory, and I don't need to be pampered. I have a housekeeper who comes in four days a week, and that's more than enough."

"And Wednesday's her day off?"

"Yeah, Wednesday's her day off."

When Tory didn't answer him, Chris asked anxiously, "Tory?"

"Yes?"

"I wondered if you were still there, that's all." He took a deep breath. "Look," he said, forcing a laugh, "if you're going out to the kitchen take me with you, will you?"

* * *

Tory settled Chris in at the kitchen table, then found a coffee maker, a tin of coffee and dealt with getting them something hot to drink first.

Then, with the aroma of the brewing coffee beginning to waft through the air, she located bread, tuna fish, some celery, mayonnaise and set about making some tuna salad to be used for sandwiches.

The fridge and the cabinets were well stocked, and she thought of fixing a warm dish for Chris. But she figured it would be easier for him to handle a sandwich, under the circumstances.

She was right. At that, he had to do a fair bit of groping, and it wrenched her heart to watch him. She was appalled by today's discovery, and she yearned to help him. Yet she didn't dare attempt to make anything easier for him than she was already doing. She saw the set pride on Chris's handsome features when he failed to connect with the handle of the coffee mug the first time around. She let him make a second effort to find it for himself, resisting the impulse to tell him the mug was just about two inches farther to the right.

It was after four and getting dark in the kitchen. Tory got up and switched on some lights and Chris, hearing the clicking sounds, immediately asked, "What was that?"

"I was just turning on some lights," Tory told him, trying to fight down a lump that was threatening to close her throat.

"Dark, is it?"

"Getting dark."

"Tory, you'd better be heading for home."

"Because it's getting dark?"

"Well, yes."

Tory forced a chuckle. "Chris, I'm a big girl. I'm used to being out after dark."

"Be that as it may...you should get along home," Chris said. "Look, I'll be okay any minute now. As it is, I'm perfectly fine. You can guide me back to that chair in the drawing room and I'll sit there till my sight comes back."

Chris spoke casually enough, but Tory, nevertheless, got the strong impression it was his stubborn pride dominating what he was saying. She knew all about stubborn pride. She had too much of it herself, as her father frequently had told her. Maybe it was easier for her than it would have been for a lot of people to recognize the signs in someone else.

"I have no intention of leaving you, Chris," she said gently but firmly.

She saw his mouth tighten. "That's ridiculous, Tory," he said.

"Ridiculous or not, I'm staying till you're okay again."

Tory picked up their mugs and dishes as she spoke and took them over to the sink. She needed some small diversionary action at the moment, even if it was only washing up a few dishes and stacking them in a rack.

She was startled to hear Chris laugh. "Suppose the curtain decides to remain down till morning?" he said mischievously.

"Then I'll stay here all night," Tory stated.

Silence thundered. Then Chris said slowly, "That's quite an offer. Please don't think me ungrateful, but I'm not going to accept it." He stood, smiled and said, "Off with you, Tory."

"No," Tory said. She hesitated, then plunged. "Look," she explained, "I wouldn't leave *anyone* alone under circumstances like this. You've suddenly... gone *blind*, dammit."

"It's a temporary condition. I've already told you that."

"All right. You still don't know how long it's going to last."

"The curtain's already beginning to go up."

Suspicious, Tory asked, "You're sure of that?"

"Yeah, I'm sure of it," Chris drawled lazily.

The lazy drawl only heightened her suspicions.

She edged toward him, moving so softly on the thick rug she was sure he couldn't hear her. She stood right in front of Chris, watching him sniff, then say, "That's a nice perfume you're wearing, Tory. And, yes, you're standing so close I could count your eyelashes...."

Tory thrust out her hands. "What color nail polish am I wearing, Chris?"

He frowned. "I guess you'd call it pink," he decided. "I'm never too great at describing colors."

"That does it," Tory proclaimed triumphantly. "I'm not wearing any nail polish. So why are you fibbing to me?"

Chris's voice was strained as he said, "Because I want you to get the hell out of here. It doesn't take psychic powers on my part for me to know this isn't about to be one of my best nights."

"And you'd rather suffer through it alone?"

"Yes."

"If our positions were reversed, would you walk out on me?"

A moment passed. Then, his voice curiously muffled, Chris admitted, "No." Impulsively, his arms went out to her.

Tory walked into them, and she let her instincts take over. She hugged him, her fingers clasped first at his nape. Then she let those fingers separate to go their own way, plunging into his thick, dark hair, and moving on to rub the back of his neck.

She leaned her head against his shoulder and could feel the steady throb of his pulse. She doubted her own pulse was even half as steady. Being so close to Chris was doing strange things to her, freeing fireflies inside her that fluttered in counterpoint to her pulse beat. Long-repressed feelings sprang free, making her intensely aware of *herself*. She didn't need to be made more aware of Chris.

Then he pushed her away, ever so slightly, and she held her breath, fearful that he was going to put an end to this magic moment between them. But instead he cupped her face between his hands, and in the next instant his lips were claiming hers as if they'd been guided by an unerring magnet.

For just a second, Chris drew back to say thickly, "You don't have to see to kiss." Then he proceeded to prove his point, except that his kiss became infinitely more than just a kiss. His kiss spoke of the things Christopher Marlowe had once written about. Just now, this other Christopher was asking her to come be his love. Communicating wordlessly, with his warm and wonderful lips, his desire, his need, and also his *reverence* for her.

Tory let the restraints that usually bound her slip away, answering his message with her own messages. Clinging to him, meshing her mouth with his, their tongues probing, touching, exploring, she rocketed with him into a new dimension. They touched the stars along the way, and since they both had their eyes closed anyway the darkness didn't matter.

Chapter Four

It didn't take visual acuity to make love, and Chris was well on his way toward proving it. In another minute he'd be unable to resist swooping Tory up in his arms, and using his memory of the house as a guide, he'd take her somewhere, probably upstairs to his own bed, where they could experience the exquisite pleasure of finishing what they'd begun.

But that kind of pleasure was not in the cards for them. Maybe sometime. Certainly not now. Chris slammed on his emotional brakes and gently, very gently, took hold of Tory's shoulders, putting an edge of distance between them.

That little bit of distance could just as well have been a vast chasm. Tory stared at him, shocked, conscious only that he was rejecting her. At once she felt flooded by a surge of humiliation, and in reaction, pride flowed through her veins.

She stepped back, hurt and ashamed. She saw that Chris was pale, tight-lipped, and it occurred to her that the gesture of restraint he'd just made hadn't been an easy one for him.

Well, why had he made it then? Going into his arms had seemed to her the most natural thing in the world. Their actions, on both sides, had been involuntarily. They'd simply yielded to what they were feeling.

Unless she had read Chris wrong.

And then there was his temporary blindness to consider. Tory's concern for him momentarily transcended her own bruised feelings. *How could I possibly think that I might be able to read his mind?*

"Tory," Chris said hoarsely.

"I think maybe you'd better sit down again, Chris," Tory said. "I could do with some more coffee, couldn't you?" She didn't wait for his answer. "I'll make a fresh pot."

"Tory, you're misunderstanding."

"What am I misunderstanding?"

"It isn't that I don't *want* to make love to you," he said. "I think we both know it wouldn't be right for either of us just now."

Tory didn't answer him. He heard water running, heard some attendant clatter, and knew she'd gone over to the sink and was filling the coffeepot again.

On the other occasions when he'd had blackouts he'd been alone. He'd managed to keep his cool; he'd ridden out the darkness. It seemed to him this spell was lasting longer than most, though he couldn't be sure about that. They all were interminable when they were happening. But he wished fervently that the damned curtain would lift so he could *look* at Tory and hopefully make her understand that he couldn't have gone to bed with her just now without loathing himself for it afterward.

She'd been so willing to give. That's why it had become so impossible to take her gift, why he had pulled back at what had come very close to becoming an ultimate moment. It would have been so wrong for him to take what she was offering, to take *her*, under these circumstances. She was a generous and wonderful person. She was upset about him—he'd sensed her concern even before today. Probably she'd been pitying him when he held out his arms to her. He detested the idea, but he had to consider it. Anyway, whatever she'd felt, this was the wrong climate in which to make love.

Chris smelled the brewing coffee and wished Tory would say something. He wished she'd accept his rationalizing and tell him she agreed with him about this not being the right moment for them.

He'd never felt so uncertain, so ill at ease. He'd never before realized how accustomed he was to being in charge, to making the decisions, to handling things in his own way. Even with women, he thought wryly.

"Here," Tory said, her voice sounding so close he was startled. "I've put the coffee mug right in front of you. There's a spoon next to it, and the cream and sugar are to the right."

"Thanks," Chris said, and felt as if he'd just been chastised.

He heard something scrape against the floor as Tory pulled her chair up to the table. The chair leg, of course. The coffee was strong, hot, just the boost he needed. After a moment he was able to say, "Tory...would you please just go along with me?"

"I'm not sure what you mean."

"I told you before...I'm not the easiest person to deal with right now. This will pass, though, and when I'm really myself again..."

"You don't need to make excuses, Chris."

"I'm not making excuses, for God's sake," he blurted. "Don't you think I wanted you?"

Seconds ticked by before she finally asked, "Did you?"

Chris smiled, and his voice was very gentle. "More than you'll ever know," he said softly.

Tory finished her coffee, then filled the mug again. She'd probably have a jangling case of caffeine nerves tonight, but right now she needed a jolt to her system to keep on going.

Everything in her urged her to get up and walk out of this house. She was only torturing herself by staying here, because regardless of what Chris was saying, she couldn't push that awful moment when he'd thrust her away from him out of her mind.

She thought back to the things Hank Chase had said about him. Chris was used to having women throw themselves at him. Hank had made that pretty clear.

Well, Tory thought bitterly, she had to face up to the fact that probably she was just another on the list. And right now, Chris, an inherently kind person, was only trying to let her down gently.

Still, regardless of that, regardless of how much she wanted to escape, she knew she couldn't leave him until she was sure he could see again.

She glanced across the table at him. He was staring vacantly into space. The terrible thought nudged. Suppose his sight doesn't come back? But he'd made it so clear that this was only a temporary condition....

"Where did you get the Pierce-Arrow?" he asked suddenly.

Tory's thoughts had never been farther from antique car restoration than they were at that moment. It took her a second to whirl things into perspective. "It belonged to a great aunt of mine who died about six months ago," she finally managed to say. "Knowing how I felt about old cars, she left it to me in her will. She lived in Pennsylvania. I had it shipped here, I didn't dare drive it without testing it out thoroughly first. It had been in a garage for years. That's why the paint job is so good." She added, "I could never have afforded to buy a car like the Pierce."

"You buy most of the cars you restore, though, don't you?"

"Yes. And the majority of them are in pretty sorry condition—cosmetically, at least. I have certain criteria when I think of buying an old car—what to look for under the hood as well as what I can obviously see," she said.

"Do you usually work on just one car at a time?"

"No. Actually there's room enough in the underground garage for me to work on three cars at a time. Right now, I'm restoring a '51 Chrysler Saratoga Coupé as well as the Pierce. The Chrysler belongs to a man in Chatham, who hired me to do the job for him."

"That, in itself, says you have to be pretty good," Chris ventured. "You spoke about an underground garage? How did you ever come by an underground garage? Did your father start with it and build your house on top of it?"

"No." Tory smiled at the memory. Acquisition of a summer house with a garage already intact had been the biggest triumph of her father's life. "My father bought the house almost thirty years ago from a man who was an old car buff," she said. "It was he who built the garage, then put his house up over it."

"You said that restoring cars was just a hobby of your father's, Tory. What did he do?"

"He was an accountant in Boston. He wanted to be a doctor, but it just wasn't financially possible. So he had to settle for a career that he was good at and did well with, but he fulfilled his dreams with the cars.

"He fixed up his first car—an old Chevy roadster—when he was a kid in high school. He had a natural talent, a natural mechanical ability, that's to say, and he took night courses as time went by. Also, he constantly studied on his own. There were always books about cars all over the place."

"What about your mother?" Chris asked.

"She died when I was born."

Chris murmured something Tory couldn't quite make out, then went on to say, "Your father must already have owned the Chatham place by then."

"Yes, he did. Actually my mother received an inheritance from her grandmother that was enough to make a substantial down payment, back then. Real-estate values were very different on the Cape than they are today. My parents bought the Chatham place, and they had two great summers there...until I was born."

"And you're twenty-eight?"

"I will be in October."

"Your father moved permanently to Chatham, and you went back to live with him after your divorce, right?"

"Yes," Tory said cautiously. She was afraid of where this conversation was going. She didn't want to get into a discussion of her marriage and its failure. Although the truth was simple—like a lot of people, she'd been unfortunate enough to choose the wrong person to team up with—she still wasn't reconciled to the fact she'd failed. She'd never been able to abide the thought of failure in anything she undertook.

She deliberately steered the conversation in another direction. "Dad had been having some cardiac problems for quite a while, but he always assured me they weren't serious. Then he had a heart attack, and after that he was forced to retire early, so he moved down here year-round.

"I had a humdrum job in Boston—working for an insurance company—and I gave it up and came down here to be with him. We had about a year together before he had the major attack that killed him. It was a wonderful year." Her voice grew lower and a little husky. "He couldn't do very much physically, but he was great at supervising. We had just finished restoring a magnificent '53 bright red Studebaker Starliner the morning of the day he died."

She didn't add that selling that car later was one of the hardest things she'd ever had to do.

"Your cheeks are wet," Chris said gently.

Tory stared at him. "You can see again," she managed shakily.

He nodded. "I told you it was just a temporary condition. I'm fine now, really I am."

"You're sure it . . . won't come back?"

"No," he said, "it won't come back tonight. These attacks are sporadic, but they don't recur that quickly."

She dared the question. "Are the doctors going to be able to do something about this for you?"

"Yes," he replied. "It's just a matter of time," he added, which was probably true, essentially, but also a considerable understatement.

He was watching her as he spoke, and wondering how he could possibly refrain from taking her in his arms again. Some of her beautiful hair had escaped from that practical bun she had twirled it into. Her cheeks were still tearstained, her gray eyes wide and as clear as rain, and questioning as she looked at him. He couldn't remember when anyone had ever been quite so concerned about him, personally concerned, and that gave him a strange feeling. It would be easy to feel indebted to Tory Morgan, and he'd never in his life been indebted to anyone. He'd even paid his dues where the advantages he'd been given by right of birth were concerned. He'd worked like hell for Kendall Boats, Inc., ever since he was a kid.

He didn't *want* to feel indebted to Tory Morgan—who was surely one of the most desirable women he'd ever met. She was so totally different from anyone he'd ever known, starting with what she did for a living and extending to her genuine caring for others, despite the fact that obviously she'd had some pretty severe bumps along her own way.

Chris looked at her and felt his temperature begin to rise. He wanted her so intensely it was all he could do to remain on his own side of the table. In about another minute he was going to need a long, cold shower. His body was urging him on while his mind was striving to keep things under control. He was only human, Chris thought wryly. Unless he took some action, fast, his body was going to win out.

He glanced at his wristwatch and forced the explanation, "I didn't realize it was so late." The words sounded trite to his ears, but they'd have to do. "Tory," he said, "this time you'd really better be getting along home."

"Yes, I guess I should," she agreed. "I have an early morning trip to Logan."

"You're going to be bushed," Chris stood as he spoke. "Come on. This time I'll lead the way."

He turned on the lights in their path, and when they came to the drawing room where Tory had left her coat, he switched on the magnificent central chandelier.

Tory nearly gasped aloud, the effect was so gorgeous. The crystals sparkled, reflecting hundreds of glittering light rays. Earlier, she'd been so preoccupied with Chris she hadn't fully appreciated the beauty of this room. It was perfection, a room that could have been photographed for a leading decorating magazine just as it was, without a single detail being changed— except for the removal of her coat and her chauffeur's cap, Tory thought whimsically. They were definitely out of place here.

She slipped on the coat, still visually appreciating the coordination of colors, the priceless antique furniture, the equally priceless paintings and the exquisite accessories that combined to make the room what it was. She saw a grand piano in a corner and wondered if anyone ever played it.

She suddenly felt very tired as she picked up her chauffeur's cap and car keys. Tired, and more than a little depressed.

"Got everything?" Chris asked.

She looked around, "Yes. I must have left my handbag in the car."

They walked across the foyer together, and Chris opened the door for her. "Back in the kitchen . . . my questions must have sounded like an interrogation to you, Tory,'' he said.

''That's okay.'' She realized he'd only been trying to pass time with his questions—and to prevent further intimacy.

Now he surprised her. ''I wanted to know more about you,'' he admitted. ''I still want to know more about you.''

He bent and kissed her squarely on the mouth. Then, ''Drive carefully,'' he said, and Tory couldn't possibly have answered him.

Tory set her alarm clock for four-thirty in the morning. She had to be at the home of the elderly couple she was taking to Logan at five o'clock. They were scheduled on an early flight to Puerto Rico, where they'd embark on a Caribbean cruise ship.

They arrived at the airport with plenty of time to spare. Tory pulled up in front of the terminal building, got out of the Caddy long enough to find a skycap to handle her clients' luggage, then bid them bon voyage and headed into Boston.

As she drove, she thought about the people she'd just said goodbye to. They'd told her that next year would mark their Golden Anniversary and they were already planning a very special trip to celebrate. They were both on the far side of seventy, but they were in fairly good shape physically and still sharp mentally, which was what counted. And they had each other. Fifty years of each other.

Tory wondered what it would be like to share fifty years of one's life with another person. She hadn't even been able to share fifty months with Randy. But their commitment, she knew now, had been one-sided from the beginning. Randy was not fifty-year husband material.

Chris came into her mind, unbidden. Could Chris stay married to the same woman for fifty years?

The question was a ridiculous one, she conceded as she found a parking place along Commonwealth Avenue out near Brighton and then went into a corner café, famous for its breakfasts. She was suddenly aware that she was hungry. All she'd had to eat since a hasty breakfast yesterday morning was the tuna fish sandwich with Chris.

She bought the morning *Globe* and read it while she consumed scrambled eggs, an English muffin and two cups of coffee. The café wasn't overly crowded this morning, and she had time to spare. She was to pick up a customer at Logan at three o'clock for a return trip to the Cape. Meantime, she planned to spend the intervening hours soaking up some culture.

The exhibition at the Museum of Fine Arts, her target for today, didn't open until ten o'clock, so she was in no hurry. She drove out along the Charles for a while, then finally reversed direction and started looking for a parking place as close to the museum as she could get—never an easy task.

The museum was featuring French Impressionists—her favorites, especially Claude Monet. Tory bought a ticket and joined the line waiting to be let into the exhibit. Firmly she told herself that for her own good she'd better start washing Chris Kendall out of her mind.

Last night they'd been thrown together in highly unusual circumstances. Otherwise, that scene in his kitchen never would have happened. He was vulnerable. He'd needed to reach out to someone, and she'd been the only person around. She—well, dammit, she'd not only been tremendously worried about him, but she'd felt a sudden physical longing for him that had been so overwhelming there was no way she could have resisted going into his embrace.

Chris Kendall was dream stuff, Tory thought as she turned her ticket over to a museum employee and moved into the exhibition area.

There were a number of Monets on view, the paintings having been loaned from other museums for this exhibit, which would eventually travel from coast-to-coast. Ordinarily seeing the beautiful paintings would have been enough to delight Tory to the exclusion of everything else. But now she was looking at original Monets and still finding it impossible to banish Chris from her thoughts.

Even some of the paintings made her think of him. She stood before *Yacht Races at Argenteuil,* a beautiful oil that had been borrowed from the Musée d'Orsay in Paris. The billowing sails on the boats looked as if they'd been painted with pure sunshine, and their shimmering golden patterns were reflected in the smooth azure water. The sailboats, needless to say, weren't Kendall Ketches. But right now, any kind of boat would have reminded her of Chris.

Tory lost track of time as she wandered around the exhibit, steeping herself in both the muted and the vivid colors the Impressionists used, and she wondered if Chris shared her enthusiasm for this kind of art. The magnificent oils in his Chatham drawing room had been of an older, more conventional school. She was sure that the painting over his beautiful, marble-manteled fireplace was a Gainsborough. Without doubt an original.

It occurred to her, as she left the exhibit and wandered back toward the place where she'd parked the Caddy, that Chris knew a great deal more about her than she did about him. He hadn't gotten the whole biography out of her last night, but he'd caused her to fill in quite a few of the gaps in what he'd already learned of her life.

He knew special things about her, too, such as her love of sixteenth- and seventeenth-century poetry. He certainly knew of her absorption with restoring automobiles from an earlier age, choice cars that, in her opinion, were so much more beautiful than the cars being made today.

The information she'd gained about him was, in contrast, very impersonal. The only really *personal* detail she knew about him was his vision problem, and that was temporary.

She wondered how he'd react if she started questioning him the way he'd questioned her last night.

But she had no intention of trying to find out. Regardless of what he said about last night, she'd seldom felt more rejected than she had when he'd gently but firmly pushed her away from him. She didn't intend to chance that experience happening again.

Chris had his world; she had hers. Last night, Tory decided, was as close as those worlds were ever going to come.

Tory's afternoon passenger was George Burton, a retired executive who now lived permanently on the Cape but still accepted consulting engagements in various parts of the world.

He'd started out as a hydroelectrical engineer, he'd explained to Tory on an earlier trip. Then over the long years of his career his native curiosity, as he put it, had led him into hydrology, which he described in simple terms as the scientific study of water and its effects upon the earth and everything connected with the earth.

The trip from which he was returning had taken him to the Canary Islands, where the water situation was critical. "But it's a terrific place," he told Tory, once they'd gone through the tunnel under Boston Harbor and she was swinging the Caddy onto the Southeast Expressway. "I'm going to take my wife back for a vacation."

"Right off the coast of Africa, you said?" Tory asked him.

"Yes. Only eighty miles, I think it is, from Morocco. The Canaries belong to Spain, though, and the overall influence is more European than African. I only got the chance to go to Gran Canaria and Tenerife, but there are several other islands, and I understand each is quite different, with its own attractions. I'd say any of them would be a great place for a honeymoon," he teased.

It was not the first time George Burton had teased her about something involving romance, and usually Tory just flipped back a quick answer. But today she could feel her throat tighten as she said, "I'm just not honeymoon minded, Mr. Burton."

"People were not meant to live alone, Tory," her passenger told her, speaking a shade more seriously than he usually did on this topic.

Was her confusion, her fatigue, showing that much? "Better to live alone than with the wrong person," she said carefully.

"True. But you're much too attractive to adopt that as your permanent personal slogan."

On an earlier trip, when they'd gotten onto a similar subject, Tory had told him she wasn't in the marriage market. "I tried wedded bliss once," she'd confessed, "and it didn't work out."

Now he said, "I've been telling Martha about you." Martha was his wife. "She wants to meet you. Suppose you might have a free night when you could share dinner with us?"

"Is Mrs. Burton a matchmaker?" Tory asked him.

"A dedicated one," he said with a chuckle.

She laughed. "I'd love to join you both for dinner some night," she said, "but please warn Mrs. Burton that I'm a dedicated bachelorette."

Once home, Tory ate an early supper—having once again skipped lunch—and discovered that she was too restless tonight to stay in and watch television. There were a couple of movies that interested her at the cinema complex in nearby Harwich. She thought of calling one of her local acquaintances and asking if they'd care to join her. Then she decided to go alone. Having someone else tag along meant having to make casual conversation, which she wasn't in the mood for.

So she drove over to Harwich, bought a big paper carton of popcorn and sat alone in the darkness of the movie house, watching figures move back and forth across the big screen as she thought, once again, about Chris Kendall.

Chapter Five

Tory spent Friday afternoon dividing her working time between the Pierce-Arrow and the Chrysler. Around four o'clock she decided to quit for a while, and was about to go upstairs and make herself a cup of tea when there was a knock at the side door of her underground garage.

Hank was one of the few people who customarily stopped by, and she was prepared to see his solid form filling the threshold space when she opened the door.

She was almost more shocked than surprised to see Chris Kendall confronting her instead.

"Hi," he said easily, and waited for her to stand aside and let him in.

She did so instinctively. Her father, being a single parent, had taken great care to instill good manners in her, and that meant making anyone who stopped by their home feel welcome. Still, after her experience the night before last, Tory had mixed feelings about this particular guest invading her turf.

Chris moved past her, and she gripped the door handle a little tighter. He was wearing a red wool parka and jeans, and she felt as if he'd taken on a different identity. The man she'd driven to Boston had stepped right out of the pages of a male fashion magazine. This man . . .

She decided she'd better not dwell on the attributes of "this man." He emanated an aura of virility, sexiness, magnetism, all items on her taboo list, especially where he was concerned.

Her eyes followed Chris as he moved across the cement floor and—simultaneously whipping off his dark glasses—came to a stop by the Pierce-Arrow.

"So this is your gem," he commented.

Tory tried to view the Pierce as if she were seeing the car from his perspective. Right now, the classic automobile didn't look all that great. The chrome trimming had all been stripped off—even the Indian with his bow and arrow had been removed, temporarily. Tory had entrusted Hank with the chrome, and he'd sent it off to be replated, choosing a place he knew near Boston where they specialized in that sort of work.

"You're seeing the Pierce at the wrong time," she told Chris, wishing she could wrap a protective blanket around the car because it just wasn't fair for such a jewel to be seen like this by someone who wasn't an antique auto buff. She couldn't expect Chris to really appreciate the Pierce, to be able to envision what the car would look like when the restoration was complete.

To her surprise, he said, "I can imagine the potential. I deal with boats, remember? They, too, look a helluva lot better once they've got all their trim on."

Tory felt slightly ashamed of herself for having underestimated him. Her father had always told her she jumped to conclusions too quickly, and this wasn't the first time she'd made a wrong assumption about Chris.

As she watched him looking the Pierce over with what certainly appeared to be genuine interest, the initial jolt of seeing him began to wear off, and she wondered why he'd sought her out. Maybe he wanted to cancel their final trip to Boston next Wednesday?

To her surprise, he ferreted a small package out of his coat pocket and held it out. "For you," he said.

Tory took the package from him, and knew at once from the feel of it that it was a book. A small book.

"Open it," Chris urged.

She discovered that her fingers were beginning to tremble as they fluttered over the plain brown paper wrapping like moths seeking light. She slowly withdrew the book, and as she read the title she couldn't repress a gasp of astonishment. It was true that she'd told Chris she liked sixteenth- and seventeenth-century poets, but even so...

What other man would ever have found something like this for her?

"Congreve," she said, fingering the gold-tooled leather binding. "It's a wonderful copy. Wherever did you find it?"

"The Friends of the Library had a book sale yesterday," Chris told her. "I saw the notice, and I hoped there might be something special mixed in with the general potpourri. I lucked out."

He grinned. "This particular volume contains 'The Old Bachelor,'" he said, "as well as some of Congreve's other works. I thought that might be sort of appropriate, coming from me."

Tory was still touching the book binding reverently. "You consider yourself an old bachelor, Chris?" she asked.

"At the moment," he said rather enigmatically, and returned to the subject of the book. "I suppose your library is loaded with Congreve," he suggested.

"No, it isn't."

"Good. You know...you're right," he said. "There's a fascination about digging into the things people wrote long ago and then discovering that so many of their phrases have made it through the centuries. I came across, 'Music hath charms to sooth the savage breast,' and Congreve also wrote what I suspect is the original version of 'Hell hath no fury like a woman scorned.' His wording is slightly different."

Tory nodded. "It's fun to find familiar quotes," she agreed, "and to discover how far back some of the sayings you considered relatively contemporary actually go. It makes me realize how little there is in the world that's really new."

Chris had wandered over to the Chrysler Saratoga. "This is a nice one," he commented. "Just about done, too, isn't she?"

"Yes."

"Her owner should be pleased."

"I hope so. My best advertising is word of mouth."

"Do you usually restore other people's cars for them, instead of sticking to your own purchases?"

"I have to take things as they come, Chris," Tory said somewhat evasively. "Look ..."

"Yes?"

"I was about to make some tea. If you'd care to join me, I'll put the tools away...."

"I'd like that," he said.

As he spoke, he knew she had no idea how *much* he'd like sharing tea with her, how much he'd hoped she'd issue some sort of invitation, so he could stay around for a while, after he'd given her the book. His common sense warned him that the most sensible course would be to limit his time with her to their Wednesday excursions to Boston. But their parting this past Wednesday had been so very unsatisfactory. He'd been tempted to make the trek over to her house late Wednesday night, but then he didn't know where she lived, and he knew it would be crazy to risk driving right after one of his episodes, especially at night.

Yesterday he'd wandered around town and found out that he and Tory lived about a mile apart. Then he'd come upon the book fair and had the good luck to find the Congreve volume. He'd tried any number of times to phone her after he got home, without success. He'd tried phoning again this morning—without success. Finally he decided he needed a mile walk across town anyway. If she wasn't home, he'd try calling her again later.

Then, approaching her house, he'd seen a two-car garage at the back of the property and the familiar pale blue Caddy parked inside it. Chris started up the front walk, intending to ring her doorbell, then thought about the underground workshop garage she'd told him about and would have bet money that's where he would find her. He'd been right.

Now he watched her as she gathered up the various tools she'd been using and started to put them away in their proper places. She had quite an assortment of tools, and he was surprised at how many of them were unfamiliar to him.

Fingering one odd-shaped strip of metal, he asked curiously, "What's this?"

Tory glanced over at the tool he was indicating. "That's a flat light dinging surface spoon," she said.

She laughed at his expression. "It's a great tool to use with a mallet or a ball-peen hammer for when you're doing surface finishing."

"What's this one?" Chris asked, pointing again.

"A low-crown radius surfacing spoon. You use it to spring-hammer reverse crown surfaces."

Chris laughed. "I think I'd better get you in a boat-yard. I'd be on much better ground."

"And I'd probably be lost."

"Not necessarily."

Tory headed toward the inside stairs that led up into her kitchen. Chris followed, and she was intensely conscious of him every step she took. The scent of him wafted upward, past her nostrils; he used a very light after-shave lotion, a clean, woodsy sort of scent. She shivered slightly. Even this much proximity to Chris was unnerving, despite all the lectures she'd been giving herself about building up a resistance to him.

At the top of the stairs, Tory switched off the garage lights and turned on the copper-clad kitchen lamp that hung over a round maple table in the center of the room. This was a real country kitchen, with a braided rug and a rocking chair under a far window and an old wood stove that she'd stoked just before she went down to the garage.

The linoleum floor was patterned so it looked like red brick. Shining copper pots hung against a white wall. Red-and-white checked curtains hung at the windows. Tory hadn't been able to resist buying a small bouquet of jonquils and pussy willows when she'd stopped at the supermarket earlier for bread and milk, and they bloomed in an old milk-glass vase in the center of the table.

Looking around, Chris asked, "Where's the cat?"

Tory had just put the volume of Congreve's works down on a small stand next to the rocking chair, and she turned to ask, "What cat?"

He smiled. "There should be a cat curled up on the braided rug in front of the wood stove, if I'm up on my traditional New England decor," he said.

She laughed. "Sometimes I've thought about getting a cat, or maybe a dog," she admitted. "But I'm out of the house so much."

"I thought of the same thing," he said. "But I'm away a lot myself, under ordinary circumstances. I've never had a cat, and I haven't had a dog since I was a kid here in Chatham, summers."

"What kind of a dog did you have?"

"A black Lab, or mostly Lab. The type they've come to call a Cape Cod dog. Matter of fact, I think that's a recognized breed, now. My good old mutt wasn't exactly one-hundred-percent pure anything, though."

Tory was surprised. She would have expected him to have had a pedigreed pet.

"We lived in an apartment in Manhattan at the time," he said. "That was just before my mother died. She didn't feel the city was the right place for that kind of a dog, and I had to agree with her. It broke my heart to part with Captain, though. Matter of fact—it was Hank Chase who inherited Captain from me. Hank pledged to let me take Captain back the next summer while I was on the Cape, but I didn't come back to the Cape that next summer. Actually I've never come back on a regular basis, since...."

Chris stopped short, giving Tory the impression that he didn't usually volunteer such a plethora of information.

As she watched, he slipped off his parka, hung it over the side of the rocking chair, then pulled out one of the kitchen chairs and sat down. Tory was starting to fill the kettle with water when it occurred to her he might prefer something other than tea.

"Would you rather have a drink?" she asked him. "I don't have a very wide range of liquor, but I do have bourbon and sherry."

"Thanks," he said, "but tea will be fine."

As she waited for the water to boil, she got out rose-sprigged cups and saucers and a hand-painted china plate on which to put some homemade cookies her morning fare had given her. Her only job today had been her routine Friday-morning assignment, which was to take Ruth Ferris, who would be eighty-one come August, around to various medical appointments, to the beauty parlor, clothes shopping, to the supermarket, or wherever Ruth happened to want to go. Though Ruth wasn't aware of it, Tory always cut the usual charge for her, paring off about a third of her customary fee. Ruth, on the other hand, always paid a little extra. One week there would be a loaf of cranberry bread, another week a pound cake, another week some pumpkin muffins, on occasions such as Thanksgiving or Christmas a special pie or cake—all of these delectable offerings baked by Ruth herself.

When they'd parted company in the early afternoon, Ruth had proffered a bag full of walnut-studded chocolate-chip cookies. Now Tory offered one of them to Chris before she put the plate down on the table, and he promptly took a bite then munched appreciatively.

"You make these?" he asked. "They're really good."

"I wish I could claim credit, but I can't," Tory said, pouring boiling water into the teapot. "A customer of mine gave them to me. She's almost eighty-one, and she can still run rings around just about anyone with her baking."

"What about you?" Chris asked her as she came over to the table with the teapot and sat down. "Do you like to cook?"

"Not especially," she admitted. "I used to cook for Dad a fair bit—anything to tempt his appetite, which wasn't all that great the last few months. But there's not much incentive to fix things when you live by yourself."

As soon as she said it, Tory wondered if that statement sounded self-pitying. She hoped not. She didn't want to give Chris the impression she felt sorry for herself because it wouldn't be accurate. Actually she felt she was just beginning to come into her own. Once she paid up the last of the debts her father's long illness had incurred and sold a couple of more of the restored cars, she'd be ready to stretch her wings. Maybe get into some local civic activities here in Chatham. Maybe travel a little...

She got back to the subject of cooking. "With all the driving jobs I have, I find it easier to eat in restaurants, most of the time, or to open up a can of something," she said.

"That's my bad habit, too," Chris allowed, again surprising her. She would have expected him to hire cooks who would be more than anxious to prepare the most exquisite gourmet dishes for his approval. "Actually I like to cook. But I usually get tied up in the office, so it's late when I get home. Like you, I stop for something on the way or open a can.''

Was he trying to communicate to her that in a lot of ways their lives weren't all that different? Tory watched Chris pick up another cookie and bite into it, and wondered if he honestly didn't know anything could be farther from the truth.

"Are you going to pour us each a cup of tea? Or hadn't it steeped long enough?" Chris asked gently.

"I'm sorry," Tory stammered quickly, and picked up the teapot.

"Nothing to be sorry about," he told her. "Incidentally, you're a devilishly hard person to get hold of, Tory."

"What do you mean?"

"I don't know how many times I tried to call you yesterday, right up to eleven o'clock at night. Then I decided it was too late to call again. I was afraid you might have gotten home and into bed in the interim and I'd wake you up."

"I was in Boston," Tory told him.

"All day and night?"

"Not exactly. I had an early run up to the airport and an engagement for a return run to the Cape in the middle of the afternoon, so I stayed in town and went to the Impressionists Exhibit at the Museum of Fine Arts."

"You like Monet?"

"I love Monet."

"Then that's one enthusiasm we share. I have a Monet in my New York condo."

Tory's eyes widened. "An *original* Monet?"

Chris wished he could say, "No, just a print," but he couldn't. The acquisition of the Monet, about three years ago, had been a kind of indulgence he rarely permitted himself. He tried to be casual, yet not too casual, as he said, "Yes... I was lucky enough to be able to get my hands on an original. It's a summertime painting Monet did in Argenteuil. There are sailboats in it..."

"I was looking at his painting of the yacht races at Argenteuil yesterday," Tory said. And added slowly, "It reminded me of you."

Their eyes meshed. Chris felt as if he were being washed in a sweet elixir by her clear gray gaze. In part because he wanted to veer away from subjects such as the purchases of original oil paintings, in part because he also wanted to keep things from getting too personal between the two of them right now, he asked, "Do you like to sail, Tory?"

"No," she said flatly.

"You've summered in Chatham all your life, and you don't like to sail?" he queried, honestly surprised.

"Yes, I've summered in Chatham all my life. But we never owned a boat. I've been sailing a couple of times but... well, I didn't like it." Tory considered whether or not to continue further, and decided to go ahead and make her admission, no matter how foolish it made her seem.

"I get seasick," she said. "I mean... I really get seasick. I get violently seasick."

She expected Chris to laugh out loud at that. Or at least to smile. Or to attempt to hide his amusement, but to fail. Instead he said seriously, "You're not alone, Tory. Lots of people get seasick. I've also known pilots who get airsick. So don't look as if you're the only person in the world who succumbs to motion sickness."

"*You* certainly must be able to stand up to rough waters in a boat," she said. "Hank mentioned you'd even been in the America's Cup."

He shrugged, "So I have other kinds of traumas. Everyone has strengths and weaknesses. The test is how you deal with them...."

"In the case of my seasickness, I just don't go on boats anymore," Tory said with a small shrug of her own.

"That's a cop-out. There's such a thing as medication, you know. Harmless medication, when taken according to instructions. A pill or two, taken a few hours before you set out on a sail, and you'd be fine." He grinned. "When the weather warms up, want to prove that?"

She shook her head. "I don't think so. Let's face it...when it comes to boats, I'm a wimp."

The fact was, she had no intention of ever boarding a sailboat—or any other kind of boat—with Chris Kendall and subsequently making a fool of herself. He'd be kind, she knew he'd be kind. But she had no intention of having him watch her turn green, and then have to hold her head as she disgraced herself. Also, she'd tried pills, once—a friend had given her some while they were sailing. The pills hadn't worked. Maybe she hadn't taken them soon enough. Even so...

"How would you feel about a drive down to Essex, Tory?" Chris asked suddenly.

"What do you mean?" she hedged.

"I had a call from my Essex boatyard manager yesterday. There was another incident the other night that could have been vandalism. Maybe kids, but more likely a reminder that our alleged saboteur hasn't forgotten us. A number of large windows were broken—rocks thrown through them.''

"That sounds like vandalism.''

"I'd agree...except there are indications that the person who threw the rocks knew his way around the yard better than vandals would. We have guards and a very good security system. He was able to elude both. He concentrated his damage on back areas, near the water. The alarm system was triggered, but by the time the cops and the guards met up with each other the perpetrator was gone. I personally think he had a boat handy, and slipped off in it.''

"Nothing was taken?''

"No. There was no attempt made to go inside.''

"Then that sounds like child's play," Tory said. "Pure malicious mischief.''

"To me," Chris told her solemnly, "it sounds like a warning.''

As Tory glanced up, startled, he said, "I've had people investigating the man we fired last fall. I'd learned he was a heavy drinker, but I didn't know much more than that about him. Now I've discovered that he was a real loner. A good worker when he was sober—he knew boats—but a rather dour and disgruntled sort of person who, as one of his fellow workers put it, went around all the time with his shoulders loaded down with chips.

"He hasn't been seen around Essex since this latest happening, but I have a strong feeling he's still in the area," Chris continued. "My investigators are probing, trying to find out all they can about him so we'll have a kind of psychological profile to go on.''

"You think he's actually unbalanced?''

"I think he's a type who's always had an ax to grind. I think maybe being fired last year because he'd caused an accident in which I was injured unhinged him enough so he's come to the point where he's primarily interested in revenge."

"But, from what you've said, you had good reason to fire him," Tory protested.

"He may not think so. Who knows what his interpretation of being fired may be, considering the type of character he is? He may consider it his personal bad luck that it was the head of the company who was injured. He may think the consequences wouldn't have been so severe if it had been someone else. In fact, he may even blame *me* for the whole thing having happened, if his mind is really warped."

"And so you want to drive to Essex?"

"Yes. I need to touch bases with my people there, I need to look things over myself, for my own satisfaction. To get the feel of the place again. I haven't been there since the accident.

"If you're willing, Tory," he said, "it'll be a two-day job. We can stay over at the old Griswold Inn. You'd like it. It's famous, historic. A delightful place."

Tory thought about staying overnight with Chris in a historic old Connecticut Inn, and wondered how she could possibly deal with being in the same place with him overnight anywhere, let alone in such a romantic setting—even if they had rooms at opposite ends of corridors on two different floors.

Chris saw the perturbed expression on her face. "No need to make a decision right now," he said hastily. "I can't make any plans for Essex until after the trip to Boston next Wednesday, anyway."

He glanced at his slim gold wristwatch. "I'd better be going," he said, and pushed back his chair. "You must have things to do."

All she had to do was face up to an evening by herself. She'd gotten used to spending evenings by herself, until she met Chris. She'd put down her loneliness to the fact that she still missed her father a great deal, even after two years.

Anyway, her social life was not *that* bereft. Now and then she went over to the Chases for supper. A couple of times recently she'd gone out to dinner with David Enfield, who was a new doctor in town. They'd met because Tory chauffeured so many of his patients around. He was young, fun to be with...but there were no major vibes strumming between them.

Not as there had been with Chris and herself, right from the beginning.

As Chris started to head for the kitchen door, she said, "You'd better go out the front way. The kitchen steps need fixing."

"I see you have a separate garage for the Caddy," he commented as she led the way out of the kitchen.

She nodded. "Yes. My underground cavern is for restorations only. The Caddy lived there for quite a while, though, while I was fixing her up."

She noticed that Chris was glancing around as they moved through her small dining room, and then into the living room, which was decorated for comfort more than anything else. The couch and the big armchair needed reupholstering, some of the wooden pieces needed refinishing. While she loved working on cars, Tory hated fixing furniture. Now, though, she tried to look at her place through Chris's eyes and decided once she sold the Pierce she'd do something about her decor.

Her house was such a contrast to his house.

Doorways, she thought a moment later, were places where moments of truth were enacted. Parting was, in itself, a termination, and at the moment of parting, subjects left unfinished needed to be rounded out.

She knew there were things to be said between the two of them, principally about the other night at his house. But she also knew that it would be best for both of them if Chris just went off into the chilly end-of-March night. She glanced at the sky. No moon nor stars tonight. It looked like rain, if not snow.

Suddenly mindful that he'd walked over here, she asked, "Wouldn't you like a ride home?"

Chris shook his head. "I need the exercise."

"It's awfully dark out."

"I have a pocket flashlight if I need to shed some light on anything."

She waited for him to say good-night. He hesitated. Then he said, "About the other night, Tory..."

"We don't have to go into it, Chris."

"Yes, we do have to go into it. My intention in coming over here was both to give you the book and to talk about the other night. I admit...talking about it isn't coming easily." He said honestly, "I'm so damned afraid I'll say the wrong thing."

"You don't have to explain," Tory said gently. "I know what you mean. I'm afraid I might say the wrong thing, too. That was an unusual time, Chris. We reacted in an unusual way because of it...."

Chris realized she was giving him an out. But he wasn't sure he wanted one.

He'd seldom felt so uncertain. He wanted very much to find the right words to say to Tory, but he wanted even more to take her in his arms and kiss her, and it took sheer force of will to keep his hands at his side. He knew that if he initiated a kiss he couldn't let it go at that. He didn't have *that* much willpower.

He also knew he couldn't wait till Wednesday to see her again.

"Tory," he asked, "would you have dinner with me tomorrow night?"

Tory had been expecting him to say, "I'll see you next Wednesday." His invitation came as such a surprise; she was taken off guard. Before she could respond, Chris pressed his advantage.

"Seven o'clock?" he suggested, then chuckled. "I guess under the circumstances, you'll have to call for me."

Chapter Six

Saturday, the weather mellowed. Tory opened her bedroom window as she dressed for her dinner date with Chris, and the air though cool, had a balmy softness and the scent of spring about it.

Outside, a new moon carved a slender crescent into the mystery of the sky, and the stars sparkled. Tory's spirits were sparkling, too. There was nothing like talking to yourself all day to make you come to some conclusions.

A long, long time ago, Philip Doddridge had written, "Live while you live...and seize the pleasures of the present day." Doddridge had died at the age of forty-nine. Maybe he seized his pleasures a bit too avidly? No, that wasn't fair, Tory thought as she picked up the atomizer that had belonged to her mother and discreetly sprayed on a little perfume. In the mid-1700s, almost fifty was a good age to live to. Back then, people died young.

Doddridge's advice appealed to her. Tonight, dammit, she was going to "live, and seize the pleasures of the present day." As she trekked out to the garage to get the Caddy, then drove across town to Chris's house, Tory remembered that when they'd first met she'd speculated about what fun it would be to play Cinderella to Chris Kendall's Prince Charming. Well, tonight she was going to let herself do exactly that. Christopher Kendall was the closest thing to Prince Charming she'd ever met, or was ever likely to meet.

Thus far, even thinking about the consequences of becoming involved with him had been enough to start all her caution flags waving . . . and sometimes she felt as though she had enough inner caution flags to line along a whole avenue. Life in general—her ex-husband in particular—had taught her to both look and think long and hard before she leaped. But tonight she wasn't going to think. She was going to thrust the caution flags out of sight for the next few hours and let herself enjoy being with the most attractive man she'd ever known. And if the Caddy turned into a pumpkin at midnight and she had to go home barefoot, symbolically speaking, having lost a glass slipper, it would have been worth it.

Chris opened the door for Tory then feasted his eyes on her before he even said hello. Her taffy-colored hair was brushed out to its full length, its ends curling gently around her shoulders. Long earrings set with brilliant green stones glittered at her lobes, the green matching the deep color of her velvet dress. She was wearing a dark cape that looked as if it might have once belonged to someone in the navy, maybe had been part of a full-dress uniform. But she'd thrown the cape back, and Chris could see the low cut of the green velvet and the way the material molded her beautifully rounded, firm breasts.

He'd noticed Tory seldom bothered with much in the way of makeup when she was working. Tonight, she'd brought out the cosmetics, but she'd used them very skillfully. The effect was pure enhancement...as was the subtle scent of her perfume.

He'd known she was beautiful, but he hadn't realized she was *this* beautiful. And she was smiling; her lips parted slightly as she looked up at him.

Chris finally found his voice. "Well, hello."

"Hi," Tory said. "My chariot awaits you."

"Want a drink for the road, first?"

"Not since I'm the one doing the driving. I didn't eat much today. If I had a drink I might go *off* the road. But if you want something, that's fine."

Chris shook his head. "It can wait."

As they went down his front steps, Tory remembered the last time they'd dealt with these steps together—going in the opposite direction, she leading him, scared to death of what was happening. She stole a glance at him. He looked very handsome, wearing a dark blue suit, a light blue shirt and a tie banded with wide stripes. And he certainly was seeing clearly enough, tonight. Looking at him, it was very difficult to believe that there might be anything physically wrong with him.

She wished she knew what his problem was, or more specifically, how dangerous it was. She assumed it had to do with his vision and stemmed from last fall's accident in his Connecticut boatyard. Yesterday, he'd mentioned for the first time that he'd been the victim of the accident that had caused the boatyard employee to be fired. Evidently it was the ex-employee who was causing trouble at the Essex yard, even though no one had actually seen him around town since these latest incidents.

Tory shivered. She didn't like the thought of a disgruntled employee out to sabotage Chris....

She hoped he'd fill in the details of the accident for her, sooner or later. But she wasn't going to lead into them tonight. Tonight, they were going to keep things light and easy.

"Where to?" she asked, once they were seated in the Caddy.

"I made reservations at the Beachside Inn," Chris said. "Is that okay with you?"

The Beachside Inn was one of the most exclusive— and expensive—places on the Cape. Tory always thought of it as a haven for rich summer people. She'd never been there herself. Until recently, the inn had been open only during "the season." The past couple of years, because of the Cape's increasing population of wealthy retirees, the Beachside had adopted a year-round schedule, and from what she'd heard dinner reservations were hard to come by, at any time.

"*Is* the Beachside Inn okay with you, Tory?" Chris asked.

"Of course," she said rather shortly.

"If there's someplace else you'd prefer..."

"No," she said.

She'd had no idea where he intended to take her. Maybe if she'd been asked her preference earlier she would have said that she'd rather go someplace less formal than the Beachside. Someplace that would be more relaxing, at least for her. She was dressed up enough for the Beachside, but she wasn't at all sure she was going to be comfortable there.

Maybe she'd had an overdose of elegance that time when she was ten when her father had taken her to Boston to have tea with her Great-Aunt Della at the Ritz-Carlton. Whatever, she liked to go to places, but a little grandeur went a long way with her.

"Have a busy day?" Chris asked suddenly.

"Not especially," she answered.

"Did you do any more work on the Pierce?"

"No. The chrome isn't ready yet. Hank was hoping the new canvas top might come in, and the canvas cover for the trunk, but they haven't. Momentarily we're halted."

"Does Hank Chase work with you a lot?"

"Just on special details—like getting the chrome done for me—and if I really hit a snag he comes over to help me out."

"He's married, isn't he?"

"Married, two children," Tory said.

"I've been meaning to drop in at the garage where he works and say hi."

"I think he'd like that."

"The years have slipped by," Chris said reflectively. "Those summers when Hank and I used to fool around together—they seem so long ago. I knew a lot of the local kids, back then. I lost touch...."

"People move in different directions, Chris."

"Yeah, I guess so."

He let the subject slide, for which Tory was personally grateful. She was very much aware of the different directions she and Chris Kendall ordinarily moved in, and that wasn't something she wanted to explore tonight. It would only diminish the joy of being with him.

It was okay to indulge in a romantic fantasy when one knew that's what one was doing, Tory told herself as she turned into the driveway of the Beachside Inn. Once past childhood, most people didn't have much fantasy in their lives; she'd had very little in hers. Nor was she about to permit herself too much because illusion's bubble could only stretch so far, and then it would break.

Right now, though, Chris was here, and she was here, and it was a gorgeous night at the edge of spring.

The trees and bushes on the grounds of the inn were strung with tiny white lights, so the whole place looked like a fairyland scene. The inn itself capped a rise of land that sloped down to Pleasant Bay. The daytime view must be fantastic, she thought. You'd be able to see clear across the bay to the outer beach, beyond which stretched the vast North Atlantic. Right now, there were white candlelights in every window of the inn, and discreetly placed floodlights highlighted the white walls of the famous old structure. The effect was spellbinding.

"Just pull up to the front entrance, Tory," Chris said. "They have valet parking."

Tory, who had been about to drive onto the parking lot and wedge the Caddy in somewhere herself, nodded. She became suddenly and acutely aware that she was about to step into Chris's world.

This was his kind of place, not hers. Would he see her in a new light in these surroundings and wish he'd never issued that impetuous dinner invitation? Was she beginning to suffer from a full-blown inferiority complex because of this awareness that the two of them moved in two different spheres? Was she already overreacting before this evening had even really begun?

A tall young man came around to Tory's side of the car and opened the door for her. As she turned the keys over to him, he eyed the Caddy appreciatively.

"What a beauty," he commented.

"Thanks," Tory said.

"Someone who knew what he was doing must have restored this for you."

Chris, who'd let himself out of the car, came up to Tory's side. "She restored it herself," he said with a smile.

"Lady," the parking attendant said, "if I had a hat I'd take it off to you."

Chris tucked Tory's arm under his and led her up the steps and inside. The moment Chris mentioned his name to the head waiter Tory could *feel* the red carpet being laid out for them.

Though the head waiter did not know Chris personally, the name registered. And deference became the order of the day. They were led to a choice table in an enormous, beautifully appointed dining room with a huge central crystal chandelier that was like an expanded version of the chandelier in Chris's house. Menus were studied and suggestions made. A wine steward came to consult with Chris, and the choice of the right wines became a serious business. Tory sat and watched, and felt totally out of place.

The wine steward departed. An appetizer of delicate seafood crepes was brought to them. Lifting her fork, Tory wondered if she'd be able to eat a bite in this environment. But the crepes were so delicious she devoured them with no difficulty.

Chris lifted his wineglass in a silent toast, and smiled across at her. And suddenly Tory was looking into his incredible blue eyes, and nothing else really mattered. She let her feelings show... and until that moment she hadn't realized just how potent those feelings were.

Dammit, despite all of her instructions to herself, despite all her determination, despite, *everything*, she was falling in love with this man. Which was absolute folly.

Was this how Cinderella felt when she tangled with Prince Charming? Although Tory had had only a few sips of wine, she was feeling slightly giddy. But she blamed the giddiness on Chris, not on the little bit she'd drunk. The way he was looking at her right now was enough to undermine her totally. His gaze was like a caress. She could feel her cheeks getting hot as his eyes swept her face, lingered on her mouth, dropped to the V of her low-cut neckline. "God, but you're beautiful," he said huskily.

Tory was staggered. She'd never considered herself beautiful. Matter of fact, she'd never given a great deal of attention to her looks. Growing up, she'd been something of a tomboy because she and her father had been such close companions. He'd taught her how to hit a baseball. They'd gone fishing together. They'd shared so much—in addition to their love of restoring old cars. Because of the nature of their activities, jeans and a shirt or pullover sweater had been her uniform, except on occasions when she had to dress up, and she'd never liked dressing up that much when she was a little girl....

"What are you thinking, Tory?" Chris asked softly.

"You surprised me, that's all."

"Because I said you're beautiful."

"I guess so."

A whimsical smile curved Chris's lips. "If you don't believe me, go take a look in a mirror," he invited. When she didn't reply, he added, "What *were* you thinking of just now?"

"Growing up," Tory said hesitantly. "How—well, how I didn't go for dolls and frilly dresses when I was a little girl. Mainly, I guess, because every time we had the chance my father and I did something together that required sturdy clothes...."

"You didn't spend all your time in that underground garage?" Chris teased.

"No, of course not."

"Where did you do most of your growing up, Tory?"

"We had an apartment in Brookline, not far from John F. Kennedy's birthplace," Tory said. "Just a comfortable sort of apartment in a fairly old building."

"Who cared for you when you were little and your father had to go off to work?"

"There was a middle-aged couple who lived down the hall from us," Tory said. "They had twin daughters who were grown, had married and left the Boston area. Grace and Albert Williams—they were such good people. Aunt Grace—I've called her that ever since I can remember—said she'd had enough of an empty nest, and she was more than willing to care for me for very little money.

"The arrangement persisted for years. Once I was in school, I'd go to Aunt Grace's apartment till Dad got home. She used to make big molasses cookies. I'll never forget those cookies and milk sessions, during which she asked me all about my day at school. Then Dad would come and get me, and we'd go over to our own place and cook dinner together. He used to think I was such a big help, but I imagine I got in his way more than anything...."

Tory's eyes misted as she thought about her childhood. Then she rallied, and decided to turn the tables. "What about you?" she asked Chris. "What was your childhood like?"

"It was great, till I was about twelve," he said. "Most of the year we lived in Manhattan. We had a penthouse on Park Avenue. It was like having your own eagle's nest. I always felt that when I went out on our roof garden I could see forever.

"Summers we'd come to Chatham. At least, my mother and I would. My father was a workaholic. He'd join us on weekends, usually came up for a couple of weeks in July or August. But then, when I was almost twelve, my mother died. Frankly I think my father didn't know what to do with me. So he sent me away to school that fall, and after that you could say I rotated from school to summer camps. I didn't spend much time at home.

"Anyway...my father remarried before very long. His second wife was a lot younger than he was, and...well, things didn't work out for him," Chris said. "They divorced about the time I graduated from prep school. My father had never been a—well, a very overt person. After the divorce, though, he really withdrew. The business became everything to him...and he worked so hard at it that it killed him."

The waiter arrived with beef Wellington. The wine steward brought a new choice of wine. Tory was abstracted as she watched the perfection of the service, her natural perceptiveness taking her beyond the things Chris had just said to her. His tone had been a shade too matter-of-fact. Obviously he felt none of the beautiful nostalgia about his childhood that she felt about hers, and for good reason.

What he hadn't said—those subtle nuances behind his words—became more important than what he had said.

Chris steered their conversation onto general, casual topics. It was clear to Tory that he didn't want to open any more doors to the past. Neither did she. This was the night for pleasure, she reminded herself, and she let herself be mesmerized, captivated by Chris's blue eyes, and his humor, and his charismatic personality.

They were finishing the last of their cappucinos when a distinguished looking gray-haired man approached their table and hailed Chris.

Clapping Chris on the shoulder, he said, "It's great to see you getting around again."

Chris smiled. "It's great to be getting around again."

He performed introductions, and a brief conversation followed before the man moved away, but Tory had recognized the name. She'd read about this man in the papers when he'd bought a place in Chatham a year or so earlier. He was the head of a major multimillion-dollar corporation and in an interview had said jokingly that he was "retiring by stages" but planned to spend as much time in his new Chatham place as he possibly could.

There'd been a genuine affection in the man's approach to Chris—and more than a little curiosity in his eyes as he'd acknowledged the introduction to her. She didn't wonder at that. Anyone Chris Kendall dated—even once—was bound to come under some scrutiny.

"How about a nightcap in the lounge?" Chris suggested. "They have a combo for dancing."

"I don't dance," Tory said.

They were walking across the lobby, and Chris came to a swift halt. "Hey, wait a minute," he protested. "What do you mean, you don't dance?"

"Just that," Tory said, aware that telltale color was creeping into her cheeks again.

"Why don't you dance, Tory?"

"Because I have two left feet."

He glanced down at her slender feet, shod in shoes that had been dyed to match the color of her dress. "They look like perfectly paired feet to me," he said, his mouth twitching with amusement.

"It isn't especially funny, Chris," Tory said sedately. "You really wouldn't enjoy dancing with me, that's all."

Chris reached over and tilted her chin upward so that she had to look at him. "Why don't you let me be the judge of that?" he suggested.

Tory could hear the music coming from the lounge. She suddenly thought of Cinderella and the ball. It hit her that this was her chance to dance with her Prince Charming, and she was not going to pass it up. If he wound up with bruised toes, that was his problem.

There was a rosy glow to the lights in the lounge, and the music was soft, old style, geared for cheek-to-cheek dancing. After they'd been given a table, Chris ordered liqueurs for both of them. Then he stood, held out an inviting hand and said, "Come on."

Tory's pulse was pounding as he led her onto the dance floor. There were not many couples dancing, and she was thankful they'd at least have some space to maneuver. Chris slipped an arm around her waist, started to lead her and right away she stiffened. He tightened his grip as they moved across the floor, as if trying to compel her to fall in with his steps, but this only made matters worse.

After a couple of minutes he said bluntly, "I feel like I'm trying to drag a mannequin around. What the hell's wrong, Tory? You're a very well-coordinated person. I've already noticed that. You couldn't drive the way you do if you weren't. So will you kindly *relax*?"

"When it comes to something like dancing," Tory muttered, "I can't relax."

He held her away from him, while still keeping time to the music, and scowled at her. "Why not?"

"I can't, that's all."

"There must be a reason."

She didn't answer.

"Okay," Chris said, drawing her close again, but she was sure he was still scowling. "Who gave you an inferiority complex about dancing?"

"My ex-husband," she said reluctantly.

"So what was he? Some latter-day Fred Astaire?"

She had to laugh at that, even though she wasn't feeling very funny at the moment. "Randy's one of those naturals at things like dancing," she said. "He was good to begin with, and when he was about eighteen his mother gave him a Christmas present of a series of dancing courses. The thing is, Randy went overboard. His steps were so intricate it was impossible to follow them—for me, anyway."

"Those kinds of dancers and their partners usually have a lot of rehearsal sessions before they take to the limelight," Chris said.

"Yes, I guess you're right. Though I never thought of it that way before. Randy expected instant performance."

"Well," Chris said, "all I expect is instant relaxation. Just let yourself go."

Tory followed instructions. She blotted out everything except Chris, and this rosy-glowed room, and the soft, sweet music. After a few minutes she leaned a little closer, Chris bent his head, their cheeks touched. When the orchestra came to a final flourish he released her grudgingly and said, "Sometimes I think the good-old days had something going for them. I'm glad there's been a comeback to this kind of dancing."

Chris clasped her hand as they walked off the dance floor together. Tory liked the feel of his strong, warm hand. She liked the feel of *him*, the way he handled things. He'd been firm but patient about her dancing, and he'd been right. She didn't have two left feet.

But she wasn't merely in danger of falling in love with Chris Kendall. She'd already fallen in love with him.

As Chris held out her chair that fact swept over Tory. She pushed it to the back of her consciousness; she'd think about it later. Think about it, think about what to do about it. Meantime, she was going to pretend she was on a cruise. She and Chris, on a cruise to nowhere. Together, living out fantasy, until the ship docked.

At her side, Chris said, "So his name was Randy?"

"Yes."

"Want to tell me some more about him?"

"Not especially."

"Does that mean you still haven't gotten over him?"

"I was over him before I divorced him," Tory said frankly. "I met him when I was working in Boston. We were totally wrong for each other, as we both found out very shortly after we exchanged wedding rings. There was nothing especially complicated about the situation. I made a mistake. I corrected it the only way I could.''

''You got the divorce?''

''It was no-fault,'' Tory said.

''Your idea, though?''

''Yes, though Randy never put up any strong objections. He wasn't a one-woman man. That was one of the main things. Aside from that, there were just too many basic things we didn't see eye to eye with. It really *was* a case of irreconcilable differences.''

The orchestra started playing again. Tory found that—incredibly—she really wanted to get up and dance with Chris again. But first she asked, ''You've never been married, have you?''

He grinned. ''I thought Hank Chase filled you in on all that.''

Before she could reply, he said, ''No, I've never been married. Marriage just hasn't been in the cards for me. I guess I can't see fitting my life in with another person's to the extent a good marriage requires. Anyway, where marriage is concerned—''

He broke off and said, ''Let's dance, shall we?''

Tory preceded him out to the dance floor, wishing that he'd finished his sentence. Even if Hank hadn't mentioned the gossip column items, she'd have known that Chris must have been involved with a lot of women in his life. Women, Tory thought glumly, probably threw themselves at him wherever he went. Yet so far he'd resisted them when it came to any serious commitment.

Why? she wondered.

What was it, ''where marriage is concerned,'' that had made Chris such a confirmed bachelor? Had he gone through an experience that had really soured him, an experience that somehow had escaped the media?

When he drew her into his arms this time, she didn't stiffen. They moved to the tempo of the music, slow music whose beat became intensely sensual. Being so close to him, feeling his warmth, her hands touching his shoulder muscles, his hand clasping her waist, made desire begin to flow like a warm current at first, but by the time the music stopped Tory felt as though she had molten lava running through her veins.

Silently, they stood in place for a long moment. Then Chris drew back slightly and looked down at her, his eyes dark and intent. She knew that he was as suffused with wanting as she was. Yet he looked . . . perplexed. And as she watched, he frowned slightly.

Tory wished fervently that she could read his mind. But she'd never laid much claim to psychic powers. When Chris said abruptly, "Let's cut out of here, shall we?" she had absolutely no idea of what was coming next.

Chapter Seven

Tory couldn't read Chris's mood as they drove back to his house. Not only was he quiet, but now it was he who seemed tense.

Had she said anything? Had she done anything? Her mind raced back over the evening, but all she'd been guilty of was asking a few questions. He'd asked as many, if not more, of her.

Regardless, some of the brilliance seemed to have gone out of the night. The moon didn't look quite so silvery, the stars had lost some of their shine. Midnight was coming early for Cinderella, Tory thought wistfully.

She pulled up in front of Chris's house, expecting to thank him for the evening, expecting him to say goodnight, and then to let it go at that. Instead he turned toward her once she'd stopped the car. His intensity was like a wave roaring in with the tide, and in the soft glow from the dashboard she could see the rigid line of his jaw.

"Tory..." he began.

Tory stared at that taut jawline, and all she could think was that the black curtain was descending again.

"Your eyes..." she said.

Chris drew a deep breath. Surprisingly he seemed to relax, or at least to begin to. His tone was wry as he said, "This has nothing to do with my eyes. It has to do only with you...and I don't know how to say it. Oh, God, Tory...I want you so much."

Tory was speechless. She'd learned something of the art of emotional camouflage, and she'd been practicing it with him since last Wednesday night...most of the time. Tonight she'd been in control until he insisted they dance. But once in his arms the sexual vibes started to hum like telephone wires in the wind, and she was thankful for the music and the people around them and even the romantic ambience. The surroundings themselves explained her response to him. The last thing she wanted Chris to think was that she might lose control again, the way she had the other night.

Now he leaned back and shook his head. "What a helluva way to put it," he said as if talking to himself. "I'm showing about as much finesse as a bull-dozer...but I could see good-night on your face. I knew in another minute that's what you'd be saying to me."

He reached over and took her hand. "Will you come in?" he asked huskily.

Midnight. Cinderella should be streaking for home before the coach turned into a pumpkin. "I don't know, Chris," Tory said slowly.

"I can't blame you...the way I suddenly blurted that out. But, look...just come in, will you? I won't push you, Tory. I think you know I wouldn't do anything you didn't want me to do. Don't you?''

"The other night . . ." she began, remembering what she still considered his rejection.

"The other night I was being a lot more sensible than I am now," Chris said honestly. "I practically wore holes in my palms, keeping my fists clenched so I wouldn't make another move toward you. You don't know how hard that was, you have no idea how hard that was. But tonight . . . tonight's different. Tonight . . . well, tonight I think we need to be together, even it's only being together for a while and nothing more."

He broke off. "Hell," he muttered, "I'm doing a lousy job of this. What I mean is, I just wish you wouldn't go right now. What I blurted out a few minutes ago is the truth. I want you. I'm certainly not about to deny that. But almost more, I want to be with you a while longer. As it is, this night is going to be so incomplete . . . for both of us . . . if you just drive away now.

"Do you know," he murmured, "right now you are absolutely irresistible?" He reached across the space that divided them and tried to draw her toward him. "Damn bucket seats!" he said with a grin. But the bucket seats notwithstanding, he bridged the distance, and his kiss was light upon her lips. He freed one hand, moving his fingers slowly over her face, carefully, deliberately, outlining her features. He paused to stroke her chin with a slow, sensuous movement. Then his fingers moved down her throat, his touch feather light, and they came to rest in the hollow of her neck. The lightness of the kiss, the lightness of the touch, made an incredible erotic combination. The molten lava began to flow again inside Tory. He'd said *she* was irresistible. What kind of comparison was he making? He certainly must be the most irresistible person in the entire world.

It was Chris who did the leading this time as they went up the steps. He'd left some lights on inside; lamps glowed in the foyer, and in the drawing room. Finally he released her hand, and smiled down at her. He looked relaxed, self-assured. It was plain to her that he'd gotten a grip on himself—whereas, inwardly, she was shaking to pieces.

"In the mood for some classical music?" he asked her.

"Yes." She nodded.

A moment later, the room was flooded with sound. Tory's father had been a classical music buff. She recognized the haunting symphony. Saint-Saëns. She sat down on a sofa upholstered in an exquisite brocade and let the music swirl around her.

She closed her eyes as she listened. When she opened them, Chris was gone. She sank back, still captivated by the music, and after a few minutes he reappeared, carrying with him a bottle of champagne and two tulip-shaped glasses.

Tory recognized the expensive label on the champagne bottle and knew it had cost more than she spent on liquor in six months. If she needed further proof of the differences in their statuses, their life-styles, the champagne none-too-subtly conveyed it to her. But this was *tonight* she reminded herself. Neither she nor Chris was about to make a lifetime commitment.

She watched him pour the golden liquid, clicked glasses with him and reminded herself that on this particular magical night it was still a long way to Cinderella's midnight, after all.

Chris sank next to her on the sofa and stretched out his legs. He loosened his tie, took it off and tossed it onto the seat of an heirloom chair. He leaned back, his dark hair brushing the brocade upholstery, and turned slightly toward Tory and smiled, a slow and easy smile.

The champagne, the music and Chris's smile were triple intoxicants; Tory felt as if both her head and her heart were spinning in a different orbit. Chris had put the bottle of champagne on a nearby table. When he reached for it and filled her glass again she protested, "I shouldn't . . ."

"You're not going anywhere," he said softly.

They clicked glasses again, and he murmured huskily, "To us, Tory. Tonight." Then before she'd taken more than a couple of sips, he took the glass away from her, and in another moment she was in his arms. At first he held her as if she were made of the most delicate china and was incredibly precious. He kissed her gently as his hands played over her breasts, her waist, the curve of her hips. But then the tempo of his lovemaking began to build like a symphony of his own composition, moving toward an inevitable crescendo.

Still, Chris wasn't hurrying what was happening between them. He wasn't hurrying her. After a while, he gave her champagne back to her, and they both drank a little more. And then he slowly drew her to her feet. "Let's go upstairs," he said. "Will you come upstairs with me, Tory?"

The staircase curved upward from the foyer to a landing where there was a red velvet loveseat beneath an arched multipaned window. Stairs verged in either direction from this central point, and Chris took Tory up the right-hand staircase, his arm around her waist, holding her to him tightly as if he were afraid she might suddenly vanish.

He led her down a long corridor and into a room she knew at once was his. The walls were stark white, the decor a blend of blues, ranging from medium to dark. The furniture was a heavy, carved wood she didn't recognize, and the bed was enormous. Chris lifted Tory as if she were as light as a bird and deposited her on a thick, soft quilt topped with pillows of varying shapes and sizes.

She giggled. "I feel like I've wandered into a sultan's harem," she said.

"Not a harem," Chris said, and added unexpectedly, "You are the only woman I've ever brought to this room."

He lay down beside her as he spoke, tugging her toward him till they were so close Tory fancied she could hear his heartbeat. He held her—just held her—but as he did, she felt as if their bodies were already beginning to merge. And when he nuzzled her nape with his lips, a flash of fire shot through her, little tendrils of flame flaring out so she would have thought she'd feel sizzling hot to his touch.

Then tenderly, reverently, he began to undress her. Before he'd gone very far, her responsiveness took over, and she started to fumble with his clothing, wanting to get rid of the buttons on his shirt, the buckle, the belt.

Chris reached out to light a single lamp on a bedside table. Its glow was soft, spreading across the deep blue quilt, spreading across *them*. In that soft light, Tory saw him—saw all of him, every inch of him—and it seemed to her that he was so perfect he could have posed for a statue by a master sculptor. She was aware that his eyes were feasting on her. She heard him mutter, "Lord, but you're beautiful,'' and she wanted to tell him he was beautiful, too, more beautiful than she was. But she'd never spoken words like those, and even now she couldn't quite manage to do so.

Still, though she might be somewhat inhibited about what she said to him, other inhibitions vanished as Chris began to caress her, stroking her slowly, sensuously. Again his touch was feather light, then his lips followed the path blazed by his fingers until the delight he was bringing Tory fired her with passion. He reached her most secret place, and she arched toward him, communicating her ecstasy by starting her fingers on their own route of exploration. She traced patterns on his firm, masculine muscles, felt the flatness of his stomach and progressed until she was caressing the very core of him, and desire became so strong that neither could resist it . . . or each other . . . for another second.

They fused, and neither time, space, the world nor the moon and stars mattered as they traveled their own way, losing themselves in each other. The music had long since stopped on the stereo downstairs, but they were playing their own music, and when the crescendo came, the universe . . . maybe several universes . . . exploded.

Tory lay within the circle of Chris's arms as the shock waves gradually subsided; she did not want to return to the here, to the now. She wanted to remain suspended with this man at her side in a place that was entirely their own. But then gradually a lovely languor crept over her, and she closed her eyes and slept, awakening only when Chris, too, awakened, and then they made love all over again.

Tory woke just as dawn's very early light was edging through Chris's bedroom windows. She turned her head, and saw Chris lying at her side, fast asleep. Slowly, inexorably, reality returned.

The clock on the bedside table told her it was nearly four-thirty. Soon it would be full daylight, and people would be stirring. She became sharply aware of her blue Caddy parked in front of Chris's house, where it had been parked all night. Not that anyone was apt to see it, she reminded herself hastily. The lane that led up the hill to Chris's house ended in a semicircular driveway. Also, his house was not only set well back, but was further camouflaged by trees and shrubs, not all of them deciduous. Anyone would really have to be looking hard to spot the Caddy, and Chris didn't have that many neighbors. The Kendall property was, in effect, a small, private estate.

Tory didn't have that many neighbors, either, at least not at this time of the year. There were several houses in her immediate area, but most of them were only occupied in summer. Nevertheless, Chatham was a small town, and people in small towns were often nosy, and inevitably they noticed things just when you didn't want them to. Also, though many people around town might not know who Tory Morgan was, her Caddy stood out. And most people knew who Chris Kendall was and where he lived, even though she doubted very many of the contemporary Chathamites had ever met him personally.

For some reason, she didn't want two and two to be put together, where she and Chris were concerned. She didn't want gossip started around town about Chris and herself.

She slid out of bed cautiously, careful not to wake him. She picked up the clothes discarded the night before, very conscious of her nakedness as she slipped out of the room and down the stairs.

There had to be a bathroom somewhere downstairs; probably more than one, she reasoned. The house was so huge it was unlikely Chris would hear the sound of running water from such a distance. It felt weird to be wandering without any clothes on through the magnificent rooms in his house. If she believed in ghosts, she'd say this prickling sensation on her skin was because long-gone Kendalls were looking down on her disapprovingly.

She found a perfectly appointed powder room off the foyer, decorated in soft tones of turquoise and lavender. She washed quickly, then slipped on the emerald velvet dress and the matching slippers and, glancing in the mirror, told herself that for this Cinderella the ball very definitely was over.

She retrieved her cape from the drawing room and, wrapping it around her, stepped outside. Spring was in the air, but so was dampness. It looked and felt as if it were going to pour any minute, and Tory scurried out to the Caddy, slipped behind the wheel and hoped Chris wouldn't hear the engine start when she turned the ignition switch.

As she drove through the quiet streets, Tory discovered she was actually praying she wouldn't meet anyone she knew. It was unlikely she would at five o'clock in the morning, but Cape Codders tended to be early risers. Once she'd put the Caddy in the garage and let herself into her house through the kitchen door, she expelled a very long sigh of relief. Before she did anything else, she filled up the coffeepot and plugged it in. She needed a jolt of caffeine.

A mug of coffee in hand, she went upstairs, showered and slipped on a comfortable robe. Then she lay down on her bed, propped her head up against the pillows and immediately contrasted her simple four-poster bed to that sumptuous, king-size affair of Chris's.

She tried to imagine what his reaction would be when he woke up to find that she'd left. This was Sunday, and he knew she didn't have any driving jobs lined up. He'd asked her about that as they were on their way to the inn last night and was glad they wouldn't have to cut short their evening because of an early commitment on her part. Now it occurred to her that maybe he'd expected they'd laze around this morning, make breakfast together, make love together....

Tory closed her eyes tightly. Their lovemaking last night had been unforgettable. What they'd shared was as perfect as sharing passion between two people ever could be. But...she could not afford a repeat performance. Her emotions were getting much too deeply involved. And, though he'd wanted her last night as much as she wanted him, sex and love were two entirely different things. If she'd learned nothing else from her marriage to Randy, she'd learned that.

Right now, Chris was temporarily out of his own circle. He'd been out of it for over five months. In the ordinary course of his life, the two of them would never have met in the first place. And even if they had, they wouldn't have been thrown together in the same way. He would have been taking someone else to dinner last night at a place like the Beachside Inn. Tory had no illusions—or delusions—about that.

Chris woke up, yawned and stretched. And without even glancing at his side, knew he was alone in his bed.

He sat up, staring around disbelievingly. He was not only alone in his bed, but he was alone in this house. He didn't need to make a safari through a series of empty rooms to verify that. If Tory was still around, he would sense her presence....

He got up and went to the window. It had started to rain, a steadily falling early spring rain. Had Tory been so anxious to get away she hadn't minded getting soaking wet, racing out to her Caddy? Or had she left before the rain began?

Why had she left at all?

Disgruntled, Chris showered, slipped on a terry robe, went downstairs and made some coffee, pausing to glance into the drawing room to see if maybe Tory had left something behind—her cape, or her handbag, or some tangible evidence of her presence. As it was, any evidence of her being here had been so totally wiped out he had the crazy feeling maybe she'd never been there at all. Maybe he'd dreamed last night.

He knew better.

He stood at the kitchen window, coffee mug in hand, staring out at the relentlessly falling rain. He swore, not from anger but from pure frustration. He knew Tory didn't have any business to conduct today; she'd told him that. So he'd made plans, intending to fix breakfast for her, as a starter. He liked to cook when he had a chance—and have someone around to enjoy his cooking—and he'd planned to fix her one of his super omelettes. According to his program, they would eat in the small breakfast room off the kitchen, which was decorated in soft yellow. It was pretty but informal, unlike the dining room, which in Chris's opinion, was banquet-and-holidays-only territory. He'd not had the occasion to spend a holiday in the house since returning to Chatham, and he was certainly not in the mood to host a banquet.

So this morning the plan had been to eat in the breakfast room, and after breakfast enjoy the day and each other.

Tory had foiled that plan, and he felt a stab of resentment. Why had she felt the need to walk out on him without a word? She could, at the least, have left a note on the kitchen table. Was she regretting what had happened between them last night? That thought was terrible, and if it was true, the letdown would be enormous. As far as he was concerned, last night had been about as sublime as anything on earth was ever apt to get. He would have sworn she felt the same way.

Was he that wrong about her?

Chris refilled his mug with coffee, sat down at the kitchen table and thought about Tory. He tried to understand what made her tick, tried to understand *her*. He knew that she was fiercely independent, loaded with pride, stubborn and unyielding about some things. But when she did yield she was the most giving person he'd ever known. He suspected that her unhappy marriage and the subsequent divorce had hit her harder than she let on. She didn't seem to be bitter about men, per se. But she gave the impression that she'd learned a hard lesson and was not apt to let history repeat itself.

She was so attractive that Chris had no doubt she must have all the opportunities she could ever want for attention from the opposite sex, and thus a well-rounded social life. Yet she gave him the impression that she primarily was a loner, and evidently she wanted it that way.

He could see that she'd given her full-time attention and love to her father during the last year she'd shared with him before his death. They'd had an unusual relationship, father and daughter, from everything she'd said. She'd actually been both daughter and son to Jeffrey Morgan, and Chris supposed that in a sense Jeffrey Morgan had probably been both father and mother to her. She'd never known her own mother, so the blow of her lone parent's death must have been a crushing one.

She'd had two years since then, to decide what she did or didn't want to do. As far as Chris could see, she wasn't tied down to anything or anybody, except maybe a classic pale blue Caddy, and an underground garage used specifically for the restoration of antique autos.

He didn't imagine her cash flow was terrific, but she appeared to be getting by without any undue hardship, and he doubted she cared very much about money anyway. On the other hand, he sensed that she did care about *his* money in a somewhat reverse way. He suspected things would be much easier between them if he hadn't inherited the Kendall fortune and wasn't the head of a large corporation.

On the other hand, he doubted very much that Tory Morgan suffered from an inferiority complex. Rather, he had the idea that she'd come to conclusions about what she liked and wanted in her life, defined her own parameters, and he was beyond her limits, through no fault of his own.

And just where did that put him?

Chris shoved back the kitchen chair on which he was sitting and went over to the window again. The damned rain was coming down in torrents, and it showed no sign of letting up. This was the kind of weather in which one should put something special on the stereo and then get comfortable with a good book...but he was in no state of mind to handle either literature or music.

He had seldom felt so confined. He thought about getting his car out of the garage—he'd had his silver-gray Porsche brought up from Manhattan after settling here in Chatham, but so far he'd resisted the impulse to drive it. The chance that if his problem occurred while he was driving, and he became involved in an accident in which someone else would be hurt, deterred him.

He thought of calling Tory and suggesting that maybe they could go over to Hyannis and catch a movie at the Cape Cod Mall. He even went so far as to start for the phone. Then he thought about her walking out of his house in the early-morning hours, and he didn't make the call.

He wondered if maybe Tory would call him with some kind of logical explanation for her action. But deep down inside, he had the feeling she wouldn't.

Tory skipped breakfast, put on some work clothes and went downstairs to the garage. She was nearly finished with her work on the Chrysler Saratoga and she knew she should put in a few hours and finish up the job. But...she just wasn't motivated.

She was at a standstill where the Pierce was concerned, because there wasn't much more she could do until the chrome came back, and the canvas top and trunk cover. Honesty compelled her to admit that today she didn't want to work on the Pierce, anyway.

She was restless and edgy and beginning to wish she'd nudged Chris into even semiwakefulness this morning to tell him she had to leave. Or that she'd scrawled a brief note explaining she had to get home and left it somewhere he'd be sure to find it.

Would he understand if she told him she'd gone off at the break of daylight because she didn't want to compromise *his* reputation, as much or even more than she didn't want to compromise her own? Though, most certainly, she didn't want to become fodder for the gossip columnists of some of the more sensational newspapers and magazines.

She wondered if maybe Chris might call, but the day wore on, and he didn't. It wasn't until she was getting ready for bed that night that it struck her how isolated he must have been today, alone in his house, unable to drive, with the rain coming down in a steady torrent.

She felt slightly ashamed, then, to think she hadn't put her pride into her pocket and phoned him to see if there was anything he wanted, or anyplace he wanted to go.

But by then it was too late to do so.

Chapter Eight

"I have good news and bad news," Hank Chase said. "Which do you want first?"

It was late Monday morning. Tory had started her day by taking an elderly man to Hyannis to keep some medical appointments then bringing him back to Chatham.

When she got home, there was a message from Hank on her answering machine saying they needed to talk. She'd driven back into town so they could speak face-to-face.

Now they were sitting in Ted Melson's tiny office, off on one side of the work bays in Melson's Garage. Monday was the owner's day off, so Hank was in charge.

Tory took a pull of the Coke Hank had just bought her, and said, "Naturally I'd prefer the good, but then I'd have to face up to the bad. So let's go with the bad, and then you can lift my spirits by springing the good on me.''

''The chrome job was lousy,'' Hank stated. ''I sent it back.''

Tory stared at him, dismayed. ''You've sent the chrome for the Pierce back to Boston?'' She didn't want to believe what she was hearing.

''Tory, this place came highly recommended, but I couldn't accept their work,'' Hank said. ''The chrome was delivered this morning. I took one look and told the guys in the truck to take it back. I called the manager up there in Boston, and I told him if he'd let work like that go out he needed a new pair of glasses. Seems his regular man has been off. He let someone who didn't have the same kind of expertise do the job. He admitted he should have checked personally before it was shipped out. He made a bad goof there. I told him there were other places where we could do business, and he got down on his knees over the phone—I could hear his joints creaking—and begged me to let him try again. He's even going to give you a ten-percent discount, for the sake of good faith, and he swears the job will be perfect if he has to do it himself.''

''But that means more time,'' Tory moaned.

''The Pierce has to be perfect, Tory.''

''Yes, I know, I know,'' she agreed. ''But . . .''

She hadn't wanted to get into the subject of her current financial situation with Hank, but there didn't seem to be any way to avoid it. ''I need to sell the Pierce, Hank,'' she said. ''I need the money.''

Hank frowned. ''You mean you need it bad?''

''Bad enough. And definitely so before much longer. I'll have the Saratoga done before the week is out, and what I get for that will help. But it won't cover everything."

"Such as what, if you don't mind my asking?"

"The house mortgage."

Hank's frown deepened. "I kind of assumed your place was paid for a long time ago."

"It was . . . almost. But when Dad retired and came down here he needed to winterize the house. He had to put in a furnace. Remember, we'd only used the house summers? Dad had to make some other repairs as well. The result was that to do everything that needed to be done Dad had to ask the bank to rewrite the mortgage. They were willing, but they gave him a variable rate mortgage. That means the interest rate fluctuates each year, either goes up or goes down."

"Yeah," Hank nodded. "I know what it means."

"Well . . . regardless of what people say about interest rates being up, down, or whatever, the interest rate has gone up annually since I took over the property, and I got a notice in the mail that it's going up again. Unfortunately I don't have enough income right now to qualify for a fixed mortgage. Not with this bank, at least, and they are people Dad dealt with for years. I do trust them.

"Anyway," Tory went on, "I'd be able to handle the added cost of the mortgage payments by cutting expenses here and there, but something else has come up."

"Such as?"

"The roof has started to leak."

Tory had made that unhappy discovery late yesterday afternoon. She'd gone up to her bedroom to get a book she was reading, and the water was dripping down from the ceiling and spattering on the floor only about a foot from her bed.

Hank glanced out the window at the rain, which was still falling steadily. "This kind of weather's enough to make anything leak," he observed. "Maybe once things dry up your leaks will dry up, too."

"Unfortunately I'm afraid it's not going to be that simple," Tory said. "There's a leak in my bedroom, the bathroom and the pantry off the kitchen. I can't remember when Dad last had anything done to the roof, so this is long overdue. But it's going to be expensive. That's why I really need to sell the Pierce as soon as I can...."

"I'd call the guy in Boston, but I hate to tell him to hurry the job," Hank said. "That's like giving trouble an invitation."

"I know." She managed a smile. "We'll do the best we can, Hank. That's all we can do."

"Hell," Hank muttered, troubled.

"Hey," Tory protested, "don't start taking this on your shoulders. It's my problem."

"And you always have to cope with your problems single-handedly, right?" Hank's tone was part serious, part teasing.

"I try to."

"You do a damned good job, too," he told her. "What bothers me, though, is..."

"Come on, Hank. Get it out."

"The good news part. It may not sound like such good news under the circumstances."

"What's that supposed to mean?"

Hank stood and stretched, then sat down again. Watching him, Tory smiled. Hank was a big, muscular man whose body demanded action. He never could sit still for very long. The ultimate horror to Hank would be having to hold down a desk job.

"Fact is," he said, "I've come upon two damned good cars you could get cheap."

Tory groaned.

"Okay," Hank said, "so this couldn't come at a worse time. On the other hand, Tory, your garage is going to be cleaned out pretty soon. First the Saratoga, then the Pierce. So when I checked out these two cars I thought to myself, Wow! What a bonanza for Tory!"

"Thanks," Tory said. "But this isn't bonanza time, Hank."

"Old cars are like the weather," Hank said. "You can't predict when they're going to come on the market. Depends on whose garage they've been parked in over the years, or whose backyard they've been rusting in. In this case, it's one of each."

"Oh?"

"A nice little old lady over in Harwich has a 1940 Ford V8 deluxe convertible coupé," Hank said.

Tory looked as if a diamond necklace from Tiffany's had just been dangled in front of her eyes. "You're kidding," she said.

"No, I'm not kidding. This lady has a big old house with an old stable in back that was converted to a garage, maybe sixty years ago. The car belonged to her husband who's been dead the past thirty years, and he kept it like it was a rare pearl. Since he died, it hasn't been out of the garage. The finish is remarkable. Even better than the Pierce's was. Shiny black, red trim."

"Richard Langworth, who's the real expert on antique cars, wrote in one of his books about collectibles that the 1940 Ford was one of the prettiest Fords ever built because of the design work by Bob Gregorie, who was the stylist for Ford at the time, and what Lang-

worth terms 'the keen aesthetic sense of Edsel Ford,'"
Tory murmured.

Hank grinned. "You quote Langworth like some
people quote Shakespeare," he said. "What a memory
you have, Tory."

She laughed. "Not really. I have sort of a freak
memory. Ask me something like a telephone number
and I'm at an instant loss. Anyway..."

"This lady would sell the car for three thousand
bucks, Tory. For the condition it's in, that's really dirt
cheap. She's going to give up her place, move into a re-
tirement home. Not immediately, but she's starting to
weed out. Tell you the truth, she used to teach English
in Chatham High years back."

"You were her student?"

"Yep," Hank admitted. "One of her worst, so she's
never forgotten me. Hell, she was old back then when I
was in high school.

"Thing is," he went on, "you buy the Ford and put
her into top condition, and I think you could get between fifteen and twenty thousand for her without too
much trouble."

"What's the other car you're talking about?"

"A Jaguar Mark II, 1960 model. And this is a crime.
The car's over in West Chatham, parked back of a garage in a weed field. It's been there too long. The Jag
belonged to a kid who picked it up relatively cheap, according to his parents, and was going to restore it himself. Thing is, the kid was going to college up in Boston,
he got into the drug scene, one night he and a bunch of
his friends were driving around and fooling around and
the guy who was driving ploughed them into the side of
a truck. The kid was killed instantly."

"Hank, that's terrible!"

Hank nodded agreement, then went on, "His parents left the car right where it was. As I say, it's been there much too long. Rust is already a bad problem that can only get worse. But at this point the Jag's still restorable. The parents have finally decided they want to get rid of it. They'd let you have it for five hundred bucks, provided you cart it out of there. Restored, you could get eight thousand for this baby, and I'd call that a minimum estimate."

"But there'd be a lot of work involved."

"Sure there'd be a lot of work involved. But that's never stopped you before, Tory."

"I know," she said. Now it was her turn to get up, and she paced restlessly back and forth in the small office, then paused to look out at the steadily falling rain.

She should have called Chris, she told herself. He was as good as a prisoner in his own house in this kind of weather. Also, the more she thought about it the more she had to admit she owed him an explanation about the way she'd walked out yesterday. The way she'd *sneaked* out, she corrected herself. As if she were ashamed of having spent the night with him, ashamed of their having made love.

What must he think?

"Tory," Hank said. "I just stumbled onto these two cars, so right now you have a first go at them. But they're new on the market, remember, and they won't be around long. They're good values. Anyone who buys them and restores them can make a good piece of change."

"I don't doubt that, Hank," Tory said solemnly, sitting down again. "If I didn't have the prospect of a new roof staring me right in the face, I wouldn't hesitate. As it is, I'm going to have to try to get a bank loan, or a home-improvement loan, to handle the roof. Right now, I'd have to do the same to buy the cars you're talking about, or else totally wipe out my savings account. We're talking about a thirty-five hundred dollar outlay. Also, it's going to cost to get the necessary stuff to restore those cars, especially the Jag. You know what I've put into the Pierce..."

"Yes." Hank nodded. "Considerable. Considerable cash, that's to say, plus God knows how many hours of labor. But you'll recoup, you'll recoup well, once you sell her."

"Yes, I know, but at best a good restoration takes a lot of time. I don't have to tell you that. I don't know, Hank. I was thinking maybe I could hold the limo service to daytime work, which is what I have principally anyway, and get a night job somewhere."

"Doing what?"

"I don't know. Waitressing, maybe. Or as a night clerk in one of the stores that stays open late. Anything, on a temporary basis, just to bring in a little extra change."

"Seems to me you've been doing pretty well with the limo business, Tory," Hank said.

"I have been. But the Caddy isn't the most economical car to run. She eats gas like a cookie monster eats cookies."

Tory sighed. "Enough. You don't need to hear any more of my problems. I'm taking off."

Hank's voice halted her. "Tory, I've got a proposition to make to you," he said. "Suppose we go partners on these two cars. You put up seventeen fifty, and I put up seventeen-fifty. Then you keep tabs of the labor and costs—clock the labor at so much per hour—and when the cars sell we'll subtract your expenses and split the profit. Meantime, I'll help you out on the labor as much as I can...."

"Hank," Tory said gently, "I appreciate the offer. I really appreciate it. But you don't have extra money to toss around, even on a good investment, unless you've been holding out on me. You have a wife and kids to think about, remember?"

"So I'll use the profits from the car sales to start a college fund," Hank said.

She smiled. "I'll think about it," she promised. "I'll think hard about it, figure out what I feel I can do and can't do, and get back to you. Okay?"

"Okay," Hank said. "But don't wait too long, or someone else is going to steal our act."

"I'll give you a call at home tonight," Tory promised as she pulled the hood of her slicker up over her head and made a dash for the Caddy, parked just outside.

The rain was showing no sign of letting up. She thought about Chris again, not that he'd ever really been out of her mind.

On impulse, she decided to make a couple of detours. Her first stop was at a deli where she bought rye bread with caraway seeds in it, braunschweiger, a good German mustard, and a large Bermuda onion. Then she slipped into the liquor store next door and bought three bottles of imported German beer, two for Chris and one for herself.

Only as she was pulling into Chris's driveway did she begin to have some qualms about what she was doing. Barging in on him like this might not be such a good idea. She wasn't sure she'd be welcome.

It was too late to reverse directions. But as she pulled to a stop in front of Chris's house, she felt a horde of butterflies flutter inside her. She gulped as she clutched the bags of food and drink she had just bought, climbed the steps and rang the doorbell.

Nothing happened.

It was a big house. A huge house. Chris could be anywhere in it. Thinking about that, Tory rang the bell again, and again nothing happened.

At that point, she started to worry. It didn't make sense that he wouldn't be home in this kind of weather. Could he have had another one of his attacks? Could he be somewhere within the house, groping around in that terrible darkness? Could he have fallen and hit his head?

Tory tried the front door. It was locked. She tried to wrap her slicker around the paper bags as well as herself as she streaked around to the back of the house, hoping that maybe she'd find a rear door that was unlocked. And she did.

The door opened into a square space that probably was used as a mudroom in weather like this. Beyond that there was a short corridor with a pantry on one side and a storage room on the other; the corridor led to the kitchen.

Tory put the paper bags down on the kitchen table, then stood very still and listened. The house was absolutely quiet.

Slowly, feeling more like an intruder with every step she took, she made her way through the downstairs rooms, and then went up the stairs to the room she and Chris had shared such a short time ago.

He'd tidied up the room, his bed was made, clothes hung up, everything had a kind of neat perfection about it.

Back downstairs again, Tory faced the fact that Chris simply wasn't here. And, only when she'd accepted that did she begin to realize what a fool she was being.

It had never occurred to her that Chris might have friends in Chatham. Not just people he'd known years ago, but wealthy people like himself.

She recalled the gray-haired man who had come to their table at the inn Saturday night. Maybe he had called Chris and invited him somewhere. Or maybe a friend of Chris's had come up from New York and they'd gone somewhere.

Maybe. Maybe.

Conjecture was getting her nowhere.

Tory left the things she'd bought on the kitchen table. Her appetite had deserted her. She pulled up her slicker hood again, and eased out the back door. Ahead of her, a wide expanse of lawn sloped downward to a gem of a pond, an almost perfect circle surrounded on three sides by pines so that if one were to sun out on the small beach at the foot of the slope there'd be absolute privacy.

Today the pond was as gray as the rain, and the wet pines so dark they looked almost black. But Tory could imagine what it would be like to share that lovely setting, and the small private beach, with Chris. They could swim together in the pond and then lie out in the sun and . . .

She firmly squelched her imagination.

Instead she focused on the three-car garage to the right of the house, built so that it looked like a smaller replica of the house itself.

Did Chris have a car here? She'd never thought about that. Could he possibly have dared to go off in a car on his own?

The thought appalled her, and she hurried over to the garage, peering through the glass panes set into the folding doors. In the dimness, she saw the shape of a car and, curious, she let herself in through a small side door and found herself facing a magnificent silver-gray Porsche.

Chris's foul-weather gear was waterproof. He was wearing a bright yellow slicker with a matching fisherman's hat and high black rubber boots. But waterproof clothing or not, after he'd been walking along the Chatham beachfront for half an hour, he felt damp all the way through.

Yesterday he'd stayed at home without the confinement getting to him too much. Matter of fact, the confinement hadn't bothered him nearly as much as Tory's actions. He'd spent the day reading, watching TV, occasionally munching on something or other, then, by evening, settling down with a snifter of brandy as he brooded about Tory.

Only his lawyer, some top people in the company, his various boatyard managers and his Boston physicians, knew his present whereabouts and had the phone number of the Chatham house. He'd wanted privacy during his stay on the Cape, and so far he'd gotten it. Now, conversely, he wished for the phone to ring, provided that when he answered it he'd hear Tory's voice at the other end of the line. But she didn't call him, and as the evening passed, Chris's own stubborn pride took over and he decided he'd be damned if he'd call her. She was the one who'd walked out.

The sight of more rain Monday morning was depressing. Chris made coffee, scrambled some eggs, watched TV news and a couple of quiz programs. But by noon, the silence, the confinement, the restlessness got to him. So he dragged out the foul-weather gear and went for a walk. The walk turned into a longer one than he'd intended. He made his way down picturesque, winding streets and lanes to Chatham Light, perched atop a bluff high over the water.

Until a few years ago, the lighthouse had faced the lower end of placid Pleasant Bay. Across the bay had stretched the barrier beach that extended all the way from Orleans to the north, to Monomoy, a wildlife refuge, on the south. Beyond the barrier beach was the vast North Atlantic.

Chris could remember boating across to the outer beach on lazy summer days. Now it still shocked him to look out from the top of the bluff at a scene that emphasized the awesome power of nature more than anything he'd ever seen.

During the course of a severe winter storm, the ocean had broken through the fragile barrier beach creating a gap that had continued to expand until now there was an aperture more than a mile in width. The result was that the sea now pounded the sand at the foot of the bluffs, and the quiet, lagoon-type stretch of bay Chris remembered was no more.

Today, he climbed the long flight of wooden steps that led down the face of the bluff to the beach, and walked along the water's edge, letting the wind and the rain buffet him. Aside from a few sea gulls, he was alone.

This communion with nature was exactly the tonic he'd needed. When finally he retraced his steps, starting back to his house, he felt refreshed—despite the bone-penetrating dampness—and considerably more in control of himself.

Then he turned into his driveway and saw the blue Caddy parked in front of his house, and he didn't know whether to be glad or sorry about this evidence of Tory's presence. Being with her would only stir things up all over again. Let Tory keep her distance, if that's what she wanted, while he kept his . . . at least until after his medical appointment this next Wednesday when his doctors would have made a decision about his case that could affect his future plans considerably.

The front door was locked, and he'd forgotten to bring a key with him, but he'd left the back door off the kitchen unlocked. He headed around the house . . . and saw a woman coming out of the small door at the side of the garage.

What the hell had Tory been doing in his *garage*? Chris halted and waited to see what she was going to do next.

Almost immediately, she looked up and spotted him, but despite the rain she made no haste in her approach to him. Her footsteps seemed to be dragging. In fact, he had the impression that she didn't want this confrontation. But in that case, why had she come over here?

Tory's pulse began to throb when she looked up and saw Chris standing stock-still, watching her. He looked as rigid as a statue. There was nothing inviting about his stance.

Well, what had she expected? An open-armed welcome after the way she'd walked out on him yesterday morning?

He waited for her to come to him. She bridged the distance reluctantly. As she neared him, looked up at him, rain spattered on her forehead, trickled down her cheeks. She brushed the errant drops away impatiently and tugged her slicker hood forward so that it better covered her face.

She saw that Chris wasn't going to make this any easier for her. He waited for her to speak, and her, "Hi," came rather weakly.

"Hi," he returned, and glanced over her shoulder toward the garage. "Did you want to borrow a tool or something? Actually I imagine you must have spares of anything I have."

"I'm sorry," she said. "I shouldn't have snooped."

An unwilling smile tugged at the corners of his lips. "Were you snooping, Tory?"

"Yes. That's to say, when I rang the bell and you didn't answer I wondered . . . well, I wondered if anything was wrong." She was damned if she was going to confess that she'd roamed all through his house looking for him. "Then I wondered if maybe you had a car and had gone off somewhere. . . ."

"I thought of going off somewhere," he admitted. "But I realized it might be a mistake to drive."

"You haven't had any more . . . blackouts?"

"No." He hadn't intended to snap the word at her, but the last thing in the world he wanted to get into with her at the moment was his eye problem. Rather he wanted to know how she felt about what had happened Saturday night.

"Well," Tory said, "I checked out the garage, just in case. I saw there was a car in there and the side door was open, so I went in. Your Porsche is a beautiful car, Chris."

"Cars do turn you on, don't they, Tory?" he observed, and added rather snidely, "maybe more than people do."

Her eyes widened. Her face became expressionless, and Chris felt ashamed of himself.

"I'm sorry," he said, and he meant it.

"No need to be," Tory said. "I shouldn't have snooped around. I only stopped by because I thought it would be hard for you to get out in the rain, and I wondered if there was anything you needed."

"Nothing, thank you," Chris said. "But I appreciate your coming by."

She nodded. "I'll be going, then," she said, and she squared her shoulders and marched toward the front of the house and the Caddy.

She didn't look back. Her eyes were filling with tears, and she hoped Chris wouldn't follow her because she didn't want him to see her cry. She got into the Caddy and turned the key in the switch and brushed the tears away angrily as the engine roared into action. But she still felt as if she was driving through a mist all the way home.

It was only when she walked into her own kitchen that Tory suddenly remembered she'd left bags full of sandwich makings and beer on Chris's kitchen table.

After Tory left, Chris walked over to the top of the slope, looked down at the rain speckling the pond and told himself that he should have put his damned pride in his pocket and gone after her.

He turned on his heel savagely and strode back to the house. As soon as he entered the kitchen, he saw the paper bags Tory had left on the table. He withdrew the contents slowly. Braunschweiger and a big onion and mustard and a loaf of bread, and three bottles of beer. Two for him, he knew automatically, and one for her.

Chagrined, he sat down at the table and wished he had the nerve to call her up and ask her to come back.

Chapter Nine

Tory didn't go straight home. She couldn't face home and solitude just then. So she drove over to Hyannis where a variety of movies were playing at the several cinemas in the malls. She went first to one movie and then to another. The second was a depressing story in which star-crossed lovers parted forever at the end. Exactly what she didn't need, she thought grimly as she drove to a Chinese restaurant over on Main Street, ordered much more than she could eat and left with a collection of white cardboard take-out cartons.

Once home she stashed the food in the fridge, then went straight upstairs. She slipped on a cotton nightgown and paused only to unplug the phone in her room before getting into bed. She hoped if the downstairs phone rang she wouldn't hear it. Right now she didn't think she could bear to talk to Chris. Both his attitude and that comment about cars turning her on had hurt, really hurt.

Her father had always said she was too sensitive for her own good. Maybe she was, especially where people she loved were concerned. And, yes, she loved Chris, God help her, and she didn't know what she was going to do about it.

Tory had an early-morning date to drive some people all the way out to Worcester, in the center of the state. They were to attend the funeral of the man's older sister, so it wasn't exactly an upbeat ride. Gloom pervaded, and the rain—down to a drizzle now, but still persisting—didn't help the overall, heavy mood.

She waited at the funeral parlor while her clients attended the service, then drove them to the home of the deceased, where friends and relatives would be gathering. She was invited to come in, but declined. Instead she drove off for an hour or so, stopped at a chain restaurant for a coffee frappé and a cheeseburger, then went back to the house and parked where her clients could spot her, and waited.

It wasn't really cold, but it was chilly and dank. The rainy day made night seem to fall even earlier. Soon the light was too dim for Tory to be able to read the paperback novel she'd brought along. She sank back and simply waited, and wished she'd studied harder in the transcendental meditation class she'd taken right after her divorce so that she could zoom in on her mantra and block out everything else.

Her clients apologized for having been so long. There had been so many relatives and friends to talk to, many of whom they hadn't seen in years. Tory assured them she'd been fine, but the three or so hour drive back from Worcester to the Cape seemed eternal, and she was exhausted when she finally got to Chatham.

After she dropped off her clients, her way home led her past Melson's Garage, and the sight of it immediately reminded her that she'd forgotten to call Hank last night about the two cars he wanted her to buy.

She was losing her memory, if not her entire mind!

She made a spur-of-the-moment decision to stop by the Chases' house and talk to Hank about the cars.

The Chases had finished their supper, and their ten-year-old son and eight-year-old daughter were both doing their homework. Tory liked Barry and Annie Chase. They were good kids, friendly kids. Now, watching them provoked a funny feeling. She wondered what it would be like to have kids. What would it be like to have a baby—her baby and Chris's baby?

That, she thought wryly, was a question that might be answered before she was ready for it. She'd taken no protective measures the other night and neither had he, which was very foolish of both of them. True, if there was anything to medical statistics, though, it had been an entirely wrong time of the month for her. But even so...

"Have a beer?" Hank invited.

"I don't think so, thanks," Tory said.

"You look pooped out." Paula Chase narrowed her dark eyes as she looked across at Tory. "Eat any lunch today?"

"Yes, I did. Honestly I did," Tory said, and managed a smile.

"Hank, give her a little of that rum you've been hoarding. Pour it over some rocks, and mix in a little water," Paula instructed. "Tory, we had tuna-noodle casserole for dinner, and there's plenty left. I'm going to heat some up for you in the micro, with a couple of veggies."

"Paula, there's no need," Tory protested. But Paula was already on her way to the kitchen.

She had to admit that the rum Hank fixed for her went down well. It was very smooth, and it gave her a nice warm sensation deep inside, where she'd been feeling pretty cold. Sipping, she said wearily, "Hank, I'm sorry I didn't get back to you last night about the cars."

"No problem," he said quickly. "Look," he added, "there's no problem, either, about my going in with you. I talked to Paula. She says we can hack it."

"I don't want you to hack it," Tory said. "I haven't gone to my bankbook and checked out the figures yet, but I will when I get home. I think if I put everything together I can get up enough cash to pay for the cars. I'll charge supplies and accessories, and anything else."

Hank stared at her, genuinely surprised. He'd told her before it wouldn't be bad business to charge what she needed for her restoration work—instead of laying so much of her limited cash on the line—and then make sure to immediately pay up all bills out of her profits. She hadn't listened to him then.

"You're right, Hank," she said, nodding at him. "This isn't just a hobby. I'm in the car restoration business. And I've come to realize, maybe a little on the late side, that not much business is done these days without some plastic money entering the picture. Anyway, I no longer intend to have such long time gaps between getting hold of a car and completing the restoration."

"How are you going to accomplish that?" Hank asked curiously.

"I'm going to work harder," Tory said grimly. "A lot harder. For starters, I have a limo service job tomorrow, but I've kept Thursday free to finish the Saratoga. I can deliver the car to the owner on Friday. That'll leave me two free spaces in the garage. If I can hire Mr. Melson's flatbed to go after the Jag and the Ford on Saturday, I'll start work on one of them on Sunday. Probably the Ford, because from what you've said it'll go a lot faster than the Jag. Also, I imagine I'll have to order materials for the Jag...."

Even as she was trying to make arrangements for getting the two venerable cars to her garage, Tory was also thinking about her casual statement that she had a "limo service job tomorrow." She *assumed* Chris still wanted her to take him to Boston for his medical appointment, but she wasn't positive.

If she did take him to Boston tomorrow, it was going to be the last time she'd be chauffeuring him. He'd booked her for three additional engagements after their first journey together. Tomorrow's trip would be the third one. In many ways, it could prove to be a real finale.

Hank broke into what threatened to become a reverie. "I'll *borrow* Melson's flatbed for you Saturday, pick up the Jag first and then the Ford. There's no reason you should pay a rental fee. Ted Melson will be glad to help you out. One of these days you can buy him a box of candy as a thank-you present. He's a nut for chocolate peppermint creams."

Tory sat up a shade straighter. "There's no need for you to spoil your Saturday off, Hank," she said.

"I'm not spoiling a damned thing," Hank assured her. "You might stop to think that there'll be the need for a little muscle in moving those cars. I'll get a couple

of the high-school kids that like to hang around the garage to learn a few tricks of the trade. You can give each
of 'em ten bucks. That'll make them happy.''

Paula came in with a tray loaded with food, which
she placed in front of Tory. Tory, glancing at the quan-
tity, was sure she couldn't eat it all. But, to her surprise, twenty minutes later she'd polished off the last
chunk of tuna and the last noodle.

She'd needed the food. She was dead tired, and she
was sure she wouldn't have bothered to eat—not even
to heat up yesterday's Chinese take-out—if she'd gone
back to her place and been by herself. She was grateful
to Paula. She was grateful to Hank. They were good
friends.

The drizzle finally had stopped. Hank walked out to
the Caddy with her. "You really keep her in top shape,
Tory," he said, surveying the pale blue car admiringly.

"I have to. She's pretty much my meal ticket right
now," Tory said.

"Look, Tory, if you want to change your mind about
my going in on the Jag and Ford with you, all you've
got to do is say so."

"I'm not going to change my mind."

"Do you ever?" he asked her.

She stared up at him, puzzled. "What do you
mean?"

"That independent streak in you is ten miles wide,
Tory," Hank told her. "Which is fine most of the time,
but other times it's a pain," he said frankly. "It's good
to be independent, but people can fall flat on their own
pride. We all need help sometimes. You're the first
person to offer help where you see it's needed, but
you're the last person to accept a helping hand from

anyone. If you're going to give, you have to learn to take some. Giving and taking—it's a two-way street.''

Hank grinned. "End of lesson," he said. "It's just that Paula and I worry about you sometimes."

Tory brooded about that remark of Hank's as she drove back to her house. She'd never thought much about give-and-take. Primarily she'd preferred giving to taking. That was simply her nature. But now Hank was telling her that she was too independent, had too much pride, maybe didn't appreciate the value of a helping hand when it was offered to her.

Was he right?

She rounded the corner onto the street where she lived, and nearly drove the Caddy up the curb when she saw Chris's silver-gray Porsche parked in front of her house.

She pulled up behind it and sat very still as she tried to slam some brakes on her mixed emotions. She could see Chris's silhouette. He was sitting in the driver's seat.

As she watched, he got out of the car and came over to her side window, which she promptly rolled down. Streetlights were sparse along her road, she couldn't see him clearly, which, at the moment, was a decided disadvantage.

"How about getting out?" he suggested.

Tory climbed out of the car, suddenly aware of the difference in their height. Right now he seemed to tower over her. She didn't need to be made to feel so small.

He followed her up the walk and into her house. She was wearing what he sometimes teasingly referred to as her "uniform," but she'd taken off the chauffeur's cap at Hank's place, and her hair spilled over her shoulders.

Up till now, Chris's expression had been stern, his face composed in what Tory privately thought of as his granite look. But his features softened slightly as he looked at her, and she wondered what she'd do if he reached out for her, took her in his arms. She was so bone weary, so mixed up about so much, she knew she wouldn't have the power to resist him.

He didn't offer her his arms. Instead he said rather curtly, "I hope I'm not interrupting any plans. I need to talk to you, Tory."

"You're not interrupting any plans." Curious, she added, "How long have you been sitting out there?"

"Too long."

"Why didn't you phone to make sure I was home?"

"I've been trying to get you on the phone. You didn't even have your machine on," Chris informed her. "I finally gave up. I decided I wanted to see you in person, anyway."

Suddenly it struck her. "You *drove*!"

"Yes," he said. "I drove."

"Chris, you know you shouldn't take a risk like that." Tory forgot about everything else as her fears for him surfaced. "Suppose you'd blacked out when you were at the wheel?"

"It's only a mile or so from your house to mine, Tory," Chris reminded her. "It takes only a few minutes to drive the distance. Also, it was raining when I left, and the streets were practically empty. In any event, when—er—when it happens, I have enough warning to know what's coming. I would have pulled over to the curb and waited for it to pass."

"You shouldn't have taken the chance," she muttered. "There's room next to the Caddy in my garage for your Porsche. You can leave it there, and I'll drive you home.''

Chris smiled slightly. "Thanks very much," he said, "but I'm not quite ready to leave."

"I didn't mean *now*," Tory protested, flustered.

Chris was wearing a beige raincoat, in lieu of the foul-weather gear she'd seen him in yesterday. He reached into his pocket and drew out a silver flask. "I filled this with brandy," he said. "I know you're not much of a drinker, but I suggest we pour some for both of us and then go sit down in your living room. As I've already said, I need to talk to you."

"I had a drink of rum at Hank Chase's," Tory protested.

"Did you eat after?"

"Yes. Paula insisted on heating up some dinner for me."

"Then I really don't think you'll have a problem, Tory. In any event, brandy's meant to be sipped slowly." As he spoke, Chris headed for her kitchen.

She followed him, knowing that she was in no state to argue with him tonight. She couldn't remember ever feeling quite so tired, and she knew her fatigue must be a combination of the physical strain driving could induce in bad weather, emotional strain over Chris and mental strain over her money worries.

"Got any brandy snifters?" he asked, putting the flask down next to her sink.

"No."

"Okay. Any kind of a stemmed glass will do."

Tory owned four wineglasses, which she'd picked up at a flea market the previous summer, thinking that sooner or later she'd want to invite someone to dinner—maybe Hank and Paula some night—and she'd have candles and flowers and serve wine. Thus far, the glasses hadn't been used, and they looked it. She washed the dust off two of them, dried them, and handed them to Chris.

Their fingers touched. An electric shock jolted through her. At least, it might as well have been an electric shock. His touch, combined with her fatigue, made her feel dizzy.

"You look beat," he said, eyeing her with concern.

Tory let herself say the words. "I am beat."

"Hard day?"

"Among other things."

"Why don't you go change into something comfortable," he suggested. "I'll take the brandy into the living room."

She thought about changing into something comfortable and shook her head. "I don't think so."

A flash of temper sparked Chris's eyes, revealing a new facet of his character to Tory. "I'm not about to try to seduce you, Tory," he said angrily.

She flushed. "I didn't think you were."

"Sure about that?" he taunted.

"Chris," she said, "please..."

He relented, picked up the two brandy-filled wineglasses and started for the living room. "Okay," he said. "But you might, at least, kick off those boots you've probably been wearing all day."

Tory followed that much of his advice. She tugged off her boots, curled up on her old couch, and it wouldn't have taken too much for her to fall asleep, despite Chris's presence.

Chris sank into an armchair and surveyed her. "What happened today to wear you out like this?" he asked her.

"It's not so much what happened it's just...things," she said, dropping her guard. "I drove some people to a funeral in Worcester, which wasn't exactly cheery. The traffic was bad on the Mass Pike. Also, it rained all the way over and drizzled all the way back, which didn't help.

"Then I stopped at Hank's because I had to give him a decision about the cars, and now I'm wondering if maybe I'm about to make a serious mistake...."

"What cars?" Chris interrupted.

"Hank's come upon a classic Ford and a Jaguar that I can get cheap," she said. "But the problem is that what might be cheap to anyone else is expensive to me, right now. I've found out my mortgage payments are going up. I've just discovered I have a leaky roof, which I'm afraid is past the point of no return. It'll have to be replaced. So to plunk down thirty-five hundred dollars for two cars I can restore may not be the smartest thing I could do right now. It'll stretch me very, very thin."

Tory was half talking to herself as she stared at the amber brandy in her glass, so she missed the change of expression that briefly transformed Chris's face.

The minute she mentioned her skimpy financial status, a warning bell clanged in his head and for just a second he froze. He'd been this route many times before. After getting to know him, so many women he'd met had told him the story of their financial needs and left question marks hanging, without actually coming out and asking him if he'd loan or give them some money.

His position on that particular issue had always been a pleasant but negative one. When it came to women and money, he was not about to follow in his father's footsteps. He'd cared a great deal for his father, admired many things about him, but he couldn't forget that an unscrupulous woman had made a total fool out of the elder Kendall, and probably cost him his life as well.

These familiar thoughts raced through Chris's mind, but then he scowled, disgusted with himself because he'd let himself think them.

This was *Tory* he was dealing with, for God's sake! Not an avaricious witch like the woman who'd been his father's downfall.

The subject was still such a tricky one for him, though, that he sounded extremely cautious as he said, "Look, Tory, I could help you out. That's to say, I'd be glad to advance you a few thousand if it would ease the burden for you."

Tory sprang to her feet, the wineglass slipping out of her fingers and shattering, the brandy spilling across the braided rug.

"Did you think I was asking you for money?" she demanded furiously.

Her vehemence astonished Chris. He felt as if he'd just been tried by a jury of one and been found guilty. For a treacherous moment, he *had* thought she was asking him for money. But only for a moment.

Tory read his expression and exploded, "I wouldn't take a cent from you if it would save my life!"

She started forward, about to run out of the room, but Chris's thundering "No!" stopped her in her tracks.

"Don't move," he ordered. "You'll cut the hell out of your feet if you take another step. Stay there while I get something to clean up the glass."

He rummaged in her kitchen closet, found a whisk broom and dustpan, and came back to find Tory standing in place, fortunately, but she was as white as a sheet and she was trembling.

In order to accomplish the clean-up job Chris had to get close to her, and he could feel the vibrations of her anger, all aimed at him. As he swept glass shards into the dustpan, his feelings were mixed. He was ashamed of his momentary suspicions, even though he'd immediately realized that those suspicions were totally unjustified. On the other hand, he didn't think he really deserved this kind of ire from her. She'd overreacted, and he was beginning to think that Tory had a habit of overreacting to anything that concerned her personally. Why was she so touchy, so sensitive? He admired independence. He admired pride, but did Tory really believe she had to battle the whole world all by herself?

Chris tried to tell himself that Tory had been speaking in anger when she'd said she wouldn't take a cent from him if it would save her life. Regardless, those words stung. Stung badly.

He surveyed the rug. As far as he could see, he'd gotten all the glass fragments, but there might still be some slivers escaping him. The light in Tory's living room wasn't especially bright.

"Where do you keep your slippers?" he asked her.

Tory's only "slippers" were a pair of well-worn leather moccasins she'd had for years. "I don't need any slippers," she said, still defiant.

"Tory, there still may be some glass slivers in the rug," Chris said patiently. "I take it your slippers are in your bedroom?"

When she didn't answer him, he impatiently muttered something under his breath and strode toward the stairs.

He didn't have to be told which of the three upstairs bedrooms was hers. Tory's room reflected Tory, but a younger Tory than the irate woman he'd left downstairs. A softer Tory.

Her furniture was maple. The bedspread and the frilly curtains at the window were pink. There were family photographs around and a variety of bric-a-brac. He was sure each piece had real significance to Tory. There was a heavily embossed silver brush-and-comb set on her dresser, which looked like family heirlooms. But what especially drew his attention was the big brown teddy bear propped up against her pillows. The bear looked as if it had been around a long time, but the pink ribbon around its neck, tied in a jaunty bow, was bright and shiny.

Chris's annoyance with Tory faded as he stared at her teddy bear. The sight of the scraggly old bear touched him, and he wished the bear could open up and talk to him and tell him all the things about Tory he so much wanted to know. He suspected the brown teddy had witnessed many of Tory's private moments. Could he become animated and speak, he would probably know more about Tory than anyone else in the world.

Unfortunately the bear was destined to remain mute. But, silent though he was, his presence demonstrated that there was a vulnerable side to Tory Chris hadn't fully appreciated until now. He could see she'd needed to become as proud and independent and stubborn as she was; but somewhere beneath the Tory she presented to the world was the warm and wonderful and giving woman who—the other night—had revealed herself to him during their lovemaking.

Chris forced his eyes away from the bear, and went over to Tory's closet. The first thing he saw was the emerald velvet dress she'd worn Saturday night. The scent of her perfume wafted from the material. Sniffing it, Chris felt a sudden surge of sharp desire, and at the same moment the knowledge hit him that he was falling in love with Tory.

The timing could not have been worse! Chris was tight-lipped as he made himself ignore the green dress and go on to the rest of the contents of Tory's closet. Her wardrobe was skimpy, and so was her supply of footwear. He saw nothing that looked like a woman's slippers to him. So he picked up a scruffy pair of moccasins that would have to do for the present, and went back downstairs.

Tory was on the couch, her feet curled under her. She still looked white and tired, her eyes were closed, and for a minute he thought she might be asleep. But as he approached her, she opened her eyes and sat up straighter, and Chris had the feeling she'd just put herself on guard again.

He held out the moccasins to her, she slipped them on. He picked up the silver flask and jiggled it. "Plenty left," he said. "I'll get you a refill."

She shook her head. "No, I really don't want anything to drink." She sighed wearily. "What was it you wanted to talk to me about, Chris?"

Chris had come here ready for a showdown. He'd wanted to know why she'd walked out on him, whether or not she regretted what had happened Saturday, why she was making herself so unavailable. Was it deliberate? Did she really want him to back off? But now the moment was at hand he didn't want to get into any of those subjects.

Logic told him that this was not a time when he should come to any far-reaching conclusions about a relationship with Tory. He had his own vulnerabilities right now. Until he worked his way through this problem with his eyes, until he straightened out the problems at his boatyards and settled the matter of sabotage once and for all, there was no way he should get involved with anyone, particularly someone who could be as easily wounded as Tory.

"What did you want to see me about, Chris?" Tory asked again, sounding even wearier.

Chris evaded the issue. "I wanted to check on tomorrow morning, that's all."

"What about tomorrow morning?"

"I thought we should leave a bit earlier than usual," Chris said, coming up with the first invention that came to his mind. "I was nearly late for my last appointment, and I don't want to chance that this time."

Chapter Ten

So much had happened during the past week. Wednesday morning Tory tried to behave as if she was about to set off on a routine chauffeuring assignment, but there was no way she could do it.

She wasn't in very good form, anyway. She hadn't needed the insistent buzz of her alarm clock to wake her up. From a sleeper's point of view, the night had been a waste.

She'd turned on her bedside radio and listened to a call-in program, which featured all kinds of people expounding on all kinds of problems while the obliging talk-show host attempted to come up with the right answers to those problems. She tried to imagine herself calling up a radio station and unloading on a stranger. Even though one's anonymity was preserved—and she could see the therapeutic benefit of getting what was gnawing at you out in the open—she had too much personal reserve, too much of a sense of privacy, to let what was deep inside her hang out like that.

Maybe Hank was right, she mused as she began to dress. Taking what he'd said a step further, she could see that maybe she'd locked herself into a mold of her own making and had become too inflexible in the process. On the other hand, this wasn't the time to start breaking out. She needed to keep herself locked up while she was with Chris today. She didn't want to give way to any more emotional outbursts, whether they involved passion, as they had Saturday night, or anger, as they had Monday night.

Chris emerged as soon as she pulled up in front of the house. They'd set their departure fifteen minutes earlier than usual, which meant he'd have time to spare once they got to Boston, unless they ran into an unexpected traffic situation on the way. But the traffic flow was normal, the volume picking up from Plymouth on toward Boston, which was routine.

Chris wasn't saying much, and he was wearing the dark glasses that masked his expression. In fact he reminded Tory of the aloof, rather grouchy man she'd been confronted with on their first trip to Boston together.

Finally she couldn't stand his silence and remoteness any longer. She had to ask, "Is something wrong?"

"Am I that transparent?" Chris answered with a question of his own.

"It's not a question of being transparent." Tory sighed. "Chris," she said, "look. I didn't mean to bring this up, but I warned you I have two left feet, and it seems like I've put them into—well, into some of the issues between us."

Chris waited.

"I shouldn't have walked out the way I did Sunday morning," Tory said, intending to say exactly that and no more. "I shouldn't—"

"Hold up!" Chris commanded. "Back to Sunday morning. Would you mind telling me exactly *why* you sneaked out the way you did?"

"I left early because I was hoping no one would see my car around your place," she said. "I might have gotten by without being recognized, but the Caddy is pretty distinctive."

Chris grimaced and asked, "Is my reputation around town really that bad?"

"No. I left when I did because I didn't want to damage your reputation," she told him.

"Are you saying *you* were trying to protect *me*?" he asked.

"Well, I wouldn't put it quite that way. I didn't want people to talk about us, that's all."

"Us?"

"Either of us," she answered.

"You didn't want your name linked with mine?"

"Actually I didn't want my name linked with you."

"God," Chris muttered, "sometimes you just don't make sense, Tory. Are you telling me *your* reputation is so bad it might damage me to be associated with you?"

"Oh, of course not," she snapped.

"Then I don't understand what you're saying." Chris sank back in the bucket seat as if resting his case.

"Look," Tory said, "All I'm saying is that Chatham is a small town and in small towns a favorite pastime is minding other people's business. You must know that. Also, you're one of the more famous citizens...."

"Come off it."

"Like it or not," she persisted, "you *are* one of the famous citizens. People respect your desire for privacy, but that doesn't mean they're not curious about you. I'd say that goes for just about everywhere, not just Chatham. Or else there wouldn't be all those gossip items—"

"You read that trash?" He sounded incredulous.

"No. No, I personally have never seen an item about you. But I've heard—"

"From whom?"

"It doesn't really matter," Tory said wearily.

"It matters to me."

"Chris...no one's told me anything malicious about you," Tory said. "I've run into a few people around town besides Hank who knew you years ago. Somehow they've found out I've been driving you back and forth to Boston—maybe Hank innocently mentioned it to someone and they mentioned it to someone else, I don't know. All they've said is that it's a long time since they've seen you, and they've asked how you're doing."

"In other words, they know about my present problem."

"No, so don't sound as if someone's betrayed you. They've just wondered how you're doing."

"Okay," Chris said. "Okay. I, personally, have run into very few of the people I knew in Chatham when I was a kid, because except for going to the barbershop and walking the beach in the rain the other day I've stuck pretty close to home. Nevertheless...I can't get over your being so concerned about my reputation, Tory."

Tory sighed again. "I didn't want a lot of talk stirred up around town about you because of me, that's all," she said. "But I guess I also wanted to get away from your house Sunday morning without being seen because..."

He had to prod her to finish the sentence. "Because *what*?"

"I didn't want to be just another name in one of the gossip column items about you."

That hit home. Chris rubbed his jaw as if Tory had actually just landed a blow on it.

I didn't want to be just another name in one of the gossip columns about you.

He couldn't blame her. He never read the kind of sensational tabloids she was talking about. He'd seen an article in a magazine in which he'd been paired with a well-known actress, but there'd been some truth to the story at the time, and in any event, it had not been unfavorable.

He decided to switch the subject. "I interrupted you before," he said. "What else is it you 'shouldn't' have done?"

"I shouldn't have become as upset as I did when you said you could let me have a few thousand dollars if it would help. But that did anger me, Chris, very much."

"I'm sorry. I'm curious, though, as to why you'd refuse to take a cent from me even to 'save your life.'"

"I couldn't, that's all."

If any other woman ever had said that to him, Chris would not have believed her. He would have been certain that she was only trying to make a favorable impression on him and her real pitch would come later.

But Tory was telling the truth. He would have staked his *own* life on that.

Maybe he was beginning to better understand where she was coming from. "Tory," he said, "I didn't mean to insult you."

"You did," she admitted, "though I know now I shouldn't have taken it that way. I know you meant well, Chris. But I also could see that the subject of money does...funny things to you."

"What do you mean?"

"You got an odd look on your face when you offered me money," Tory said. "Wary, suspicious. When I calmed down later and started thinking about that I realized why."

"Why?"

"Well, people like you must have all sorts of demands made on them by other people who are greedy or unscrupulous or both."

People like you.

Was she *trying* to widen the gap between them?

Chris opted for the truth. "You're right about people tending to make demands on other people who have a little more than they do," he said. "And I agree that money does strange things to people. Both to people who have it and to people who don't have it." He paused. "I don't negate the merits of having it," he went on. "And it's trite to say that having money isn't everything, though it isn't. What I *am* saying is that whether a person does or doesn't have money shouldn't matter so much. Unfortunately in our society it does."

Chris stared out the car window as he continued. "I can imagine the hell it must be to have to face up to unpaid bills every month, to get deeply in debt because of family illnesses, or for one of many other reasons. That's a problem I've never had to deal with. But I've had to deal with other problems, some of them just as heavy—"

He came to an abrupt stop. "I'm getting off track," he said.

"No," Tory contradicted. "What you're doing is giving me a different slant. I can begin to understand how you must have felt when you thought I was coming on to you for a loan."

Exasperated, Chris said, "I did not think you were coming on to me for a loan. For a second, some old, old hang-ups surfaced. But only for a second. For God's sake, Tory, if I know anything about you, it's that you're neither grasping or conniving and you certainly don't ask any favors of anyone.

"I suppose you'll bite my head off for bringing this up, after a moment," he added, "but...are you going to be able to manage handling your added financial problems and buying those two cars Hank has found for you, too?"

"In answer to your first question, I won't bite your head off," she said with a slight smile. "And, yes, I'll be able to manage getting the cars. I'll have to work harder, that's all, which won't hurt me."

"Work harder?" He didn't like the sound of that. "Don't you work hard enough?"

"Most people could, maybe should, work harder," she evaded. "I need to put more time on the restorations so I get them done faster. Hank will be scouting other cars for me, and when I finish the Jag and the Ford I'll want to buy maybe three others and start on them right away. I think the limo service is solid enough at this point to qualify for a bank loan, if I need one. Anyway...the main thing is to keep my production going and to get the work done. Naturally I won't sacrifice quality. That's the last thing I'd ever do. Also, Hank can help me out when he has some free time from the garage and not too much that's pressing at home.

We're going to establish an hourly wage that's fair and take it back from the profits..."

Tory saw that Chris was frowning, and she decided to change the subject. "So why don't you tell me your problem?" she asked him.

His frown deepened. "What do you mean?"

"Well, we just finished talking about me," she pointed out.

The frown turned into a very slight smile. "Tit for tat, eh?"

"Well?"

He shrugged. "There's been another incident at the Essex boatyard," he said. "This time there's not much doubt it's sabotage."

"What happened?"

"Two of the boats that were nearly completed were vandalized. Ed Simmons, the Essex manager, says it looks like a madman climbed aboard each of them and took a hatchet to everything that could be axed.

"Ed says it's obvious this was done by someone who knows his way around the yard," Chris continued, the frown returning. "No kid stuff, in other words. We've hired a new team of private investigators, and they're canvasing the area. Gus Burke, the man we fired last fall, has been spotted a couple of times—one in a liquor store, late at night just before the place was to close up, another time in a supermarket. The detectives tried to follow him, but he got away. He was using a motorcycle for wheels. A big one. They couldn't get close enough to be sure of the make. On the basis of all this, the cops have issued a warrant for Burke's arrest. Problem is to locate him so the warrant can be served. He's very slippery, very crafty."

"I'd say he's also dangerous."

Chris shot a glance at her. "You sound like Ed."

"He said this man Burke is dangerous?"

"He's thought so all along. Burke was a good worker in his day. Then he started to have domestic problems. His wife left him, ran off with another man. He began to drink. Not a new story. Burke managed to cover up the drinking pretty well, though, or he would have been out of the yard long before the accident happened. He's a big man; he can handle a fair share of alcohol...."

"Just what did happen last November, Chris?" Finally Tory dared to pose the question to him.

"I drop in at the different boatyards from time to time for an unannounced inspection," he said. "Nothing formal about it. I have faith in the management at each of the yards. I just like to know what's going on.

"Last November I hit Essex in time for lunch with Ed Simmons. We ate at a seafood restaurant near the boatyard. It was one of those bright, late fall days you still get once in a while in November. Bare trees, but the sunshine was brilliant. I particularly remember the sunshine because it was some time before I saw it again.

"I insist that anyone who's going to be around the yard wear a hard hat," Chris said, "and I follow my own prescription. If I hadn't had a hard hat on, I would have been killed. As it is...we were at the finishing stages on a yacht that had been commissioned by a man whose name you would recognize instantly if I were to tell it to you. I was abreast of the yacht at the same time Gus Burke started up a side ladder. He was carrying a gallon can of varnish with him. The decks are finished by hand, varnished, rubbed down, revarnished—"

He broke off. "I'm straying. To tell you the truth, Tory, I'm still not very keen on talking about this. The accident was a freak thing. It never would have happened if Gus hadn't been drinking. He was unsteady, it didn't take much for him to lose his balance. The can of varnish slipped out of his grasp. I was in the wrong place at the wrong time. Everything happened so fast there wasn't even a chance for anyone to shout a warning.

"The can struck me on the head. Even the blow was...freaky. The edge of the can struck the edge of the hard hat I was wearing. The hat was knocked off, but the major impact was deflected. I still was knocked cold. They rushed me to an area hospital. I had a bad head gash—my hair covers the scar—a severe concussion and several other assorted injuries that finally necessitated ophthalmological surgery."

"You said you didn't see the sunlight for quite a while."

"Yes. I lost track of time. One hour, one day, rolled into another. I still don't know exactly how long it was before I could see again. In the interim, everything was...dark charcoal. Then my sight began to come back, and it came back fully. But the terrible headaches that had been a major reason why the surgery had been undertaken began to recur."

"And you still get the headaches?"

"Yes," he admitted grudgingly. "I like to think they're not as frequent as they were, but I still do get them."

"That's why you're making these trips to Boston? The doctors are trying to do something about the headaches?"

"Basically," Chris said. "Now can we talk about something else?"

Tory didn't want to talk about anything else. She wanted to talk about him. But she knew better than to persist. So for the remainder of the ride to Boston, they delved into a broad range of subjects, discovering that they both liked baseball, that Chris liked ice hockey, she didn't, and that she liked to watch golf matches, which, he said, bored him, though he appreciated the excellent coordination and expertise involved in being a top pro golfer.

As Tory was pulling up to the Commonwealth Medical Medical Complex, Chris said, "I don't know just how long I'll be. Why don't you take your time and roam around, and I'll do the waiting for you this time."

"Maybe," Tory hedged and watched him stride, once again, toward the glass front doors of the medical building. Though he hadn't come out and said so, she had the strong feeling that today was decision time for him, and she wanted to be around once the doctors were through with him.

She put the Caddy on the hospital parking lot and went into the lobby. She'd forgotten to bring along her usual book of poetry, so she settled for a couple of the magazines lying around on side tables. But mostly she idly thumbed the pages. She was thinking too much about Chris to concentrate on what she was reading.

It was nearly noon when he appeared. He was wearing the dark glasses, and Tory could read nothing from his expression.

"Ready to go?" he asked her. Then as she nodded and stood he noticed the magazine she was holding. "What," he exclaimed in mock horror, "no Dryden or Milton or Chaucer or Swift today?"

She shook her head, troubled. His cheerfulness seemed forced, and she felt sure he was trying to cover things up.

They reclaimed the Caddy, and as Tory was pulling out of the parking lot Chris suggested stopping for lunch.

Tory merely nodded. But once they were on the Southeast Expressway heading out of the city, she couldn't stand it any longer. "What happened?" she asked bluntly.

"Not too much," Chris evaded.

"Chris, will you kindly tell me what happened back there?"

"The initial surgery was successful," Chris said.

"So?"

"A subsequent problem arose."

"What kind of problem?"

"Okay," Chris said tersely, "I'll say this once, fast, and then let's not talk about it anymore. In addition to the other injuries, I had a skull fracture last fall. Everyone thought it healed well, but now it seems that subsequently there's been a slight leakage of cerebral fluid and that's what's causing the headaches and the blackouts.

"At first it looked like this would mean more surgery. Very serious surgery. That's what the doctors have been contemplating this past month. But they've come to the conclusion that the condition should respond to laser treatment, which is infinitely simpler. I'll go in next week, and I shouldn't be laid up long."

"Next week?"

"The sooner the better, as far as I'm concerned."

Tory tried to put herself in his shoes. Probably she'd feel the same way, she conceded. Nevertheless, by the time they reached the restaurant in Braintree, whatever appetite she might ordinarily have worked up was conspicuously absent.

She ordered a salad but could only toy with it. Chris, on the other hand, polished off a steak sandwich, two cups of coffee and a slab of apple pie.

Then they were back on the road. "Tory?" Chris suddenly said.

"Yes?"

"I mentioned our taking a trip down to Essex so I could check out the boatyard situation myself. Ed Simmons is going to come up Friday, so he'll be able to update me on what's going on currently at the yard as well as to give me the latest information about Burke. Who knows? By then maybe they'll have caught up with him and he'll be behind bars."

Chris continued, a shade too casually. "Ed is going to stay on and go to Commonwealth with me on Monday. So...everything's taken care of."

He was leaving her out completely. That was Tory's first reaction. Now that he had a crisis looming, he didn't want her around any longer. Tory gritted her teeth so she wouldn't flail out at him verbally.

It was hard to remain silent, though. She wanted to ask him how he expected her to just wash him out of her mind and then go on about her daily business as if he'd never invaded her heart. Didn't he realize that it was going to be hell for her to stay behind while he went to Boston for this surgery? Didn't he know that she wanted to be with him every minute, that she wanted to do all sorts of stupid things like hold his hand when he was in pain, and soothe him when he was worried?

Was he really that indifferent to her feelings?

This time it was she who decided that they needed to talk.

They turned off the highway and headed over to Chatham. "Would you care to take potluck tonight?" Tory asked casually.

For a moment she thought Chris hadn't heard her. Then he said, "Excuse me. I was...sort of off in space. What did you say?"

"I asked if you'd like to take potluck at my house. I have the makings for sloppy joes and a salad."

"Thanks very much, Tory," he said, "but I think I'd better ask for a rain check. I need to get home and start making some phone calls. I'll give you a ring tomorrow...."

Tory merely nodded and said, "Okay," and didn't bother to tell him she was booked a full day tomorrow. She had back-to-back trips to Logan, and she wouldn't be getting home until very late.

She pulled into Chris's driveway and came to a stop in front of his house. He looked at her for a long moment, but he was still wearing the damned dark glasses, so she couldn't see the expression in his eyes. She felt totally frustrated as he leaned over and kissed her lightly on the lips. She wanted to grab him and kiss him back and put everything she was feeling into that kiss. But she didn't.

At the door of his house, Chris turned, smiled at her and waved. Tory waved back then left as fast as she could without making the Caddy actually burn rubber.

This was the second time Chris had rejected her. And the second time, she was discovering, hurt considerably more than the first had.

Chapter Eleven

Ed Simmons arrived in Chatham early Friday afternoon. "Did you have lunch?" Chris asked as they bypassed the drawing room and headed toward the library.

Ed nodded. "I stopped for a fried clam roll in a place the other side of the Bourne Bridge."

"Okay, then. Coffee? Coke? Or a drink?"

"Nothing right now," Ed said. "Let me talk myself dry, first, then maybe I'll go for a bourbon and soda— even if the sun hasn't gotten over the yardarm, as we nautical types put it."

Ed was a small, wiry man in his early fifties. His hair had silvered prematurely, and his eyes were a clear, light blue. He'd been with Kendall Company ever since his graduation from a New Haven high school, working his way up to his present position, which was one of considerable authority demanding a great deal of knowledge. The company had been good to him, and he was loyal to it.

"Shall I begin with a progress report—or do you want to get into the matter of Gus Burke, first?" he asked Chris.

"Let's have the progress report first," Chris said. He smiled. "Something tells me the Essex yard's in such good shape, aside from these sabotage incidents, it won't take long for you to fill me in."

"It shouldn't," Ed admitted. And it didn't.

But all the time Ed was talking, Chris had his mind half on what his boatyard manager was saying and half on Tory. He'd tried to get her on the phone from mid-morning yesterday until midnight. By the time he'd left the fifth message on her answering machine, he wondered if she was avoiding him, or if she'd really been out that long.

Ever since she'd let him off at the house Wednesday, he'd been trying to forget the expression on her face as he got out of the car. She'd made him feel like some kind of Judas. Then he'd thought she was going to take the edge off his driveway as she swerved the Caddy around the curve and streaked out into the street.

His feelings had been incredibly mixed during the course of that whole drive back from Boston. He wanted to reach out to Tory, to tell her that he wanted her by his side every minute, from right then till he walked out the hospital door. But he recognized his own vulnerability, and he didn't want to burden Tory. It wouldn't be fair. She had enough problems of her own to handle. She didn't need his added to her burden.

Once he was out of Commonwealth, once they had Gus Burke behind bars, then maybe he could explore his feelings for Tory. He wanted to come to her without burdens.

In the meantime...

He heard Ed say, "I think that's just about it."

"Sounds good." Chris nodded, not having heard the last part of Ed's report at all.

"On to Burke," Ed said, and then hesitated. "Chris, I think I could use that bourbon and soda about now."

"Fine," Chris said. "I'll even join you." But as he went out to the kitchen to make the drinks he was wondering what was bothering Ed so much about the Burke situation that he'd go for an afternoon drink. Ed was an extremely temperate man.

Once back in the library, he waited for Ed to bring up the subject of Gus Burke. But Ed stalled, first sipping his drink, then twirling the ice around, then sipping again.

"Okay," Chris said, alerted. "What's the problem?"

"We've put on a couple more private eyes."

"That's a problem?"

Ed shook his head. "The reason we needed the extra men is that there's a chance Burke may be heading for the Cape, if in fact he isn't here already."

Chris stared at his boatyard manager. "What makes you think Burke's come here?"

"The head of the new detective agency we've hired is an ex-New York City cop, and he's quite a psychologist," Ed explained. "So, it turns out, is one of our local police lieutenants. The two of them have been theorizing together. Take it for granted, for the moment, that Burke is our arsonist-saboteur. They reason that since he isn't getting any feedback from the vandalism at the Essex yard he's probably getting impatient. Which means either he's already moved on, or is about to.''

"And you're so certain he'll come to the Cape?"

"We all think so, Chris," Ed said reluctantly. "It makes sense. After Burke got fired last fall, he disappeared from sight. We still haven't found out where he holed up for over three months. Maybe he was right around Essex somewhere—maybe he was off in another part of the country. We haven't been able to track down any friends or relatives. If the man has relatives, we don't know about them. If he has friends, we can't find them. The private eyes did locate and talk to his ex-wife. She hasn't seen Burke in over a year, and she appears to be the last person who'd give him so much as a drink of water.

"We figure he was probably alone for those three months. Our detective reasons that during this time Burke was licking his wounds. Could be that for a time he laid off the liquor and actually tried to pull himself together. But then...the resentment began to set in. Probably he started drinking more heavily than ever, and the combination was potentially lethal."

When Ed fell silent, Chris advised, "Keep going."

"The experts feel he blames you for his losing his job. Also, there's little chance he would ever get another job in a boatyard anywhere. He might have tried that in the beginning, but it's certainly too late now. The word would get back to us. We'd blacklist him.

"So what has he been living on all this time? Under the circumstances, he couldn't have put in for unemployment compensation. Our experts think he had a cash hoard. That seems the most logical explanation. Also, who knows? Maybe lately he's taken to stealing.

He's clever, quick, as sly as a fox, all of which, combined with his motivation, makes him dangerous.''

"His motivation?"

"He hates your guts, Chris," Ed said frankly. "I think we can accept that as fact. As I've already said, he blames you for having lost his job. Also, according to our private eye, he probably blames you for the accident."

"*What?*"

"We're dealing with someone who's pretty unhinged at this point," Ed said. "If he was approaching paranoia to begin with, he's becoming increasingly paranoid all the time. As you know, we've kept the sabotage attempts in the boatyard under wraps. The police have been very cooperative. Nothing has leaked to the press, for example. Burke has yet to have the satisfaction of picking up a paper and reading about his latest attempt to get back at you. Ditto listening to a radio program, or watching TV. There's been absolutely nothing about anything that's gone on.

"Maybe we've been wrong *not* to come out in the open." Ed mused. "Because it begins to seem like what we've done has only increased Burke's discontent and his desire for revenge. Which means that the next step is likely to be a personally directed vendetta against you."

"And you think that's why he's coming to the Cape. He knows I'm here?"

"I'm afraid so," Ed said heavily. "We're all afraid so. Last time he broke into the yard—the night he hacked up the two boats—he also got into my office and went through papers I'd left on my desk. There were notes of a phone conversation I'd had with you that day, Chris. I'd jotted down your number here in

Chatham so I could get back to you about something—I don't remember exactly what it was, in any event it doesn't matter. I know your number here's unlisted. But just having the exchange digits would show him that it's a Chatham, Massachusetts number, and that would be a big first step."

Ed finished his drink and set down the glass. "I don't like this," he said frankly.

Chris frowned. "I'm not crazy about it myself," he admitted. "Look, Ed...let me get one thing clear. Do all of your 'experts' actually think my life is in danger?"

"Very possibly," Ed said solemnly. "Both the private eye and the police lieutenant have worked out a very thorough profile on him. They've talked to everyone in the yard who worked with him, everyone in town who knew him even slightly, and that's about all anyone did know him. Also, they've filled in the information about him his ex-wife gave our men."

"And?"

"The consensus is that he's out to pay you back, to make you suffer, but that doesn't mean he's out to kill you. It also doesn't mean that your life's *not* in danger, because this is not a rational man we're dealing with. Whatever Burke thinks up can easily boomerang. That's to say he may have no intention of doing severe bodily harm to you or anyone else. But if you're in the path of whatever he's up to, another accident could happen."

Chris listened to this, let it sink in. And as he did so, the realization that he was not the only one in possible danger began to grow. Suppose Burke really was on the Cape; suppose he'd been hiding out right here on the property when Tory came by Wednesday in the Caddy. He would have observed the car, he would have observed Tory. Tory had said the Caddy was distinctive; it wouldn't be too hard to pin down Tory's Limousine Service and to ask a few innocuous questions around town about Tory, herself.

Chris tried to tell himself it was farfetched to think that Burke would latch on to the personal relationship between Tory and himself. But even that was not impossible. Suppose, for instance, he somehow stumbled onto one of the waiters who'd served them the other night at the Beachside Inn. Anyone seeing them together, Chris thought suddenly, would have known they were pretty much immersed in each other....

"Ed, do you have a picture of Burke?" he asked abruptly.

Ed's eyebrows lifted in surprise. "With me? No?"

"There has to be one at the boatyard. He had to have been photographed when we hired him."

"In making their inquiries, the private eyes and the cops had been using the pic that was taken when Burke was hired," Ed said. "It's a good likeness, though it goes a few years back and he's heavier and looks a lot more dissipated now than he did then. But anyone would recognize him from it."

"I need it," Chris said. "Matter of fact, I need five or six copies. But one copy especially, as soon as I can get it."

Ed hesitated. "If you're planning on circulating Burke's picture around town, I wouldn't," he advised. "This is a small town. If Burke is here, he'd catch on to the fact his picture was being shown around and he'd skip. Our one chance of getting him is to keep a low profile and use the element of surprise. That's why the two agency men will be in town tomorrow morning. They're holing up at a small inn over on the main street.

I know April is not exactly the tourist season on the Cape, but they'll fade into the general picture. They're good. Very good."

"All right," Chris said. "You can skip getting me five or six copies of Burke's photo but I still need one."

"Why?" Ed asked.

"Because there's one person I really do have to show it to."

At four o'clock on Friday afternoon, the owner of the Saratoga picked up his car, and wrote Tory a check for her work on it. Then he departed in high style, loudly singing her praises while his wife drove the family car behind the venerable Chrysler.

He certainly was a client worth pleasing. He belonged to an area club of antique car owners, and there were few antique car owners who would stop at possessing one vintage auto if they could possibly afford another. This man would pass the word around about her, and his endorsement should prove good for some future business.

Tory looked at the Pierce, still bereft of its chrome trim, and wished for the hundredth time that *that* particular foul-up hadn't happened. Otherwise, she could put in a couple of more hours of work right now.

Instead she went upstairs, made herself a cup of tea and set about deciding whether to do some housecleaning or simply relax and maybe read a book or watch TV.

As she was leaving the kitchen, the phone rang. She didn't expect to hear Chris's voice. She assumed he was tied up with the boatyard manager from Essex. When he asked, "Tory?" she couldn't immediately answer, and he had to repeat her name.

Only then did she say, "Yes."

"I think you must be the hardest woman in the world to get hold of," Chris complained. "I lost track of how many times I tried to call you yesterday."

"I had two round-trips to Boston," she said.

"Will you be free tomorrow night?" Chris asked her.

She hesitated. "Hank's bringing over both the Jag and the Ford tomorrow," she said.

"Yes, I know that. I do have a memory, Tory."

"I didn't mean to imply you didn't. It's just that I thought you were..."

"You thought I was what?"

"Too occupied with other things."

Chris swore under his breath. Then it occurred to him they were actually quarreling; at least coming closer to an open quarrel than they ever had before. Though he couldn't have spelled out his rationale for thinking so, this seemed a healthy sign.

He nearly blurted out something like, "I'm never too occupied with other things to think about you," but hastily substituted, "You don't plan to start work on the cars the minute they arrive, do you?"

Maybe he would have done better with the first line, he thought when Tory rejoined, "I plan to start work on them as soon as I possibly can."

"Well, I wish you'd hold off long enough to come over here for dinner tomorrow night," Chris said.

Tory had been stunned at hearing his voice on the phone. Now she was stunned all over again. She said, "I thought you were busy with your boatyard manager from Essex."

"Ed is here, yes," Chris acknowledged. "I'd like you to meet him. He has the kind of know-how with boats that you have with cars. Aside from that, there's something I need to show you."

When she didn't immediately answer, Chris pressed his advantage. "Seven o'clock?" he asked her.

"All right," Tory said, having lost the opportunity to think of a reason to say no.

Despite her present financial condition, Tory was sorely tempted to get something new to wear to Chris's for dinner. But she resisted the impulse, settling for a simple beige dress she'd had for several years, which still looked good when dressed up with a little jewelry.

She slipped on a red, all-weather coat, then set out for Chris's. As she drove, she told herself she *could* have started restoring the Ford tonight and probably should have. The coupé was a real beauty and in such good condition the restoration should be relatively simple. The Jag was more of a challenge but eventually would be well worth all the effort she was going to have to put into it.

Hank had delivered the cars, the Ford first, then the Jag. She'd offered him a beer, and he'd hung around long enough to drink it and to give each car a brief inspection.

It was nearly six when Hank left. She had to shower and dressed hastily. As she pulled up in front of Chris's house, Tory was wishing she'd had a little more time to fool with her hair and makeup. As it was, she felt she looked rather plain tonight.

Chris's eyes immediately told her otherwise. He held nothing back in both his appraisal and his approval of her. Then he tossed her coat over a chair in the foyer, and led her not into the drawing room, but into the far-cosier library.

She immediately liked Ed Simmons. She liked him even more as the evening progressed, and she noted

Ed's attitude toward his boss. He not only respected Chris, but he obviously had a genuine affection for him and was not afraid to tease him when an opportunity arose.

When Chris announced that he'd cooked their dinner, Tory wondered what they were about to eat. He'd said he liked to cook, but she couldn't imagine his actually ever having done much of it.

The mushroom caps stuffed with lobster he served as an appetizer were evidence that Chris knew how to blend seasonings to create a terrific flavor. They were followed by a delicious beef Stroganoff with an accompaniment of rice and assorted vegetables, then an endive salad, and then an impressive dessert—flaming peaches over ice cream.

"I've always said if you ever wanted to get out of the boat business you could get a job as a chef," Ed Simmons observed as he sipped a cup of after-dinner coffee.

"Don't tempt me." Chris grinned, but he sobered as his eyes fell on Tory.

He and Ed Simmons exchanged glances as Tory watched. Then Ed said, "Would it be all right if I use the phone in my bedroom? I'd like to give my wife a call."

"By all means," Chris said.

They'd dined in the breakfast room, then gone back to the library to have coffee. Now, once Ed had left the room, Chris went over and sat behind the beautiful cherry desk, opened the top drawer and took out a flat manila envelope.

"This was sent up from Connecticut by courier earlier today," Chris said, tapping the envelope. "I don't want you to keep it—I wouldn't want it to be found in your possession. But I do want you to take a very good look at the photo I'm going to show you. I want you to be sure that if you ever actually see this man you'll recognize him."

Mystified, Tory stared at the large, black-and-white glossy photograph Chris held out to her.

"I'm sure I've never seen this man," she said, studying the photo.

"I didn't think you had," Chris said. "And I hope you never do. But as I've said, you need to memorize his face, just in case. If you happen to see him around town, get to the nearest phone and call the cops. Let them take over."

Tory stared at him. "Who is this man, Chris?"

"Gus Burke. Ed has reason to think he's on the Cape or, if he isn't, he may be shortly. Two private detectives from the agency that's representing us are already on the scene here. The local police are cooperating with the Essex police," Chris added. He hadn't intended to tell her that, but knowing Tory as he did, he knew he needed ammunition to convince her that Burke was bad business. Very bad business.

"In the latest sabotage incident, Burke damned near got caught," he said. "We figure the night watchman must have been within seconds of discovering him. So he ran. He dropped the hatchet he'd been using. His fingerprints were all over it. That's all the evidence that was needed to convince the authorities, as well as Ed and myself, that Burke definitely has been responsible for all the incidents that have been happening. So he's not someone to fool around with, Tory. Matter of fact, I'm relieved the night watchman *didn't* catch him. To this point, Burke has never gone beyond sabotage attempts—vandalism, arson in a couple of cases. But if he'd been cornered, who knows what might have happened? He would have had the advantage of surprise. He might have attacked the watchman with the hatchet...."

"Why has he come to the Cape?" Tory asked, even though she was already pretty sure of the answer.

"To get even with me," Chris said simply. "Thing is, I won't be around for a while, come Monday. I'll be in the hospital in Boston. The house has a good security system. I doubt Burke could penetrate it. Also, the local cops will be keeping a close watch around this place, and the two private eyes we've hired will be keeping their own watch all around town."

"Have you circulated this picture of Burke locally?"

"No. The pros feel that to do so might have an adverse effect. Someone who saw the picture might tip off Burke, inadvertently. Ed agrees with that. So we have only this one copy brought up here today by courier. I felt you had to see what Burke looks like."

Chris tried to tell himself that there was only the slimmest of chances his disgruntled employee would ever make a connection between Tory and himself. But where Tory was concerned, he couldn't bear to take even the slimmest of chances.

Ed Simmons wandered back into the room. "All's well at my home base," he said with a smile.

Chris was glad for the interruption. He didn't want to frighten Tory needlessly by verbalizing the nagging fears for her safety that kept prodding him. If she did what he'd asked—if she happened to see Burke and at once got in touch with the police—she'd be in no danger. Though Burke might be somewhat unbalanced at this point, it was very doubtful that he was actually insane.

"How about my getting us all liqueurs?" Chris suggested. "Grand Marnier, Sambucca, Benedictine? I think there's a fairly good assortment on hand."

"Benedictine would be fine with me," Ed said, and settled down in one of the leather armchairs.

"You, Tory?"

"Yes, Benedictine would be fine." She spoke absently, her mind on the man whose picture Chris had put on top of the desk. If Burke had actually made the trek to the Cape, his vendetta was very serious.

She was actually glad that Chris would be going to Boston on Monday.

Ed Simmons waited until Chris was out of earshot, and then said, "I take it he showed you Burke's picture."

Tory nodded. "Yes."

"If you do happen to see Burke, don't take any chances with him, Tory," Ed cautioned. "There's no telling what might push him over the edge."

"That's what Chris inferred," Tory said. She knew her worry was showing, wondered if some of her feelings for Chris were showing, as well. She'd already concluded that Ed Simmons was a very perceptive man.

He verified that when he said softly, "Chris is a great guy. He's remarkably down-to-earth, remarkably unspoiled, considering his background. When he first came into the boatyard to work summers, when he was just a kid, I thought, 'Oh, no...here's daddy's little rich kid, and we're going to have to treat him with fur-lined kid gloves.' But it wasn't like that. Chris wanted to learn the business, wanted to learn every aspect of it. He worked shoulder to shoulder with men more than twice his age.

"His real talent, though, lies in design. I would say that he is one of the best boat designers to come along in a long time. He tends to give most of the credit to his grandfather's original design, where the Kendall Ketch is concerned. Actually the present boat reflects about ten percent of the original and about ninety percent of Chris's ingenuity. But you'd never get Chris to admit that."

Ed smiled. "He'd have my neck for telling you that," he said cheerfully. Then sobering slightly, added "Normally I wouldn't. Enough people gossip about Chris, people who don't even know him. He tosses off the talk, but I know it gets to him. Once he said that being gossiped about was like having mosquitoes buzzing around and biting you. anyway, Tory..."

Their eyes met, and Tory liked everything she saw in Ed's face, in his clear blue gaze. "I'm telling you this," Ed said, "because I've been watching you and I think you care. Genuinely care. About Chris himself, not about any of the trappings."

She couldn't answer.

"I also think," Ed continued, "that it works both ways, or Chris wouldn't have shown you Burke's picture. He wouldn't have invited you over here to dinner. He's my employer, true. But the two of us have a kind of special relationship. I'm flattered to say that I think he wanted me to meet you."

Chris appeared in the doorway, carrying a tray with a bottle of Benedictine and some small stemmed glasses on it, and Ed made an off-the-cuff remark about the Cape, as if that was the subject he and Tory had just been discussing.

As they sipped the liqueur, Chris and Ed took over the conversation, for which Tory was grateful.

The time came to leave. Tory said goodbye to Ed, and gave him an impulsive hug. When she turned to also say goodbye to Chris, he quickly said, "I'll walk you to your car."

There was a moon, tonight, and polished stars, and a soft April breeze wafted in from the land side of the Cape, so it had spring warmth to it. The post lamp at the end of the front walk spilled radiant light over the yellow crocuses and early red tulips that edged the property. Some of the magic that had been missing lately stirred within Tory and with it a sweet, heady surge of desire.

Chris walked around to the driver's side of the car. Moonlight shafted across his face, and she could see that he looked grave. It struck her anew that he had a lot to face up to next week, and she wished he'd let her face up to it with him. But she knew he wouldn't. He'd already made that clear.

He's even more stubborn than I am, she thought rather sadly.

"Well," she said, "I guess I won't see you before you take off Monday."

"No," he said.

"Would you—would you ask Ed to call me and tell me how everything goes?"

"Yes," he said.

He seemed to be restricting himself to words of one syllable, and she wanted more than that. "Chris," she began, but before she could go on speaking he took her in his arms. For a moment he just held her so close she could feel the rise and fall of his breathing. Then he kissed her, and he put everything he was unable to say into the kiss.

When he finally released her, he laid a cautionary finger on her lips before she could speak.

"Later," he said.

Later. Tory looked up at him, and wished she could believe in later.

Chapter Twelve

The chrome for the Pierce was brought down from Boston Monday morning. Hank inspected it as closely as if he were viewing germs through a microscope and pronounced it perfect.

Later in the morning, the canvas top and the trunk cover arrived. Tory called Hank, and he came over on his lunch hour so he could inspect those items, too.

"Now you can get going and finish up the Pierce," Hank said as he sat at the kitchen table wolfing down the huge ham-and-cheese sandwich Tory had made for him. "I'm going to put the word around that shortly there'll be a real beauty for sale. I also think you should do some advertising. Wouldn't hurt to advertise in the Chatham paper, as a starter. There are a lot of rich people around here. Then there are the Boston papers, and some special outlets. But I think she'll go fast, Tory."

"I hope so," Tory said, and she did . . . on one level. She needed the money the Pierce would bring. But on another level, she hated to part with the car. It was the most beautiful car she'd ever worked on, and she never expected to have another like it. Also, in her mind it was somehow mixed up with Chris. Maybe because he'd shown such a genuine interest in her work on it.

She wished she could afford to give it to him. The color of the car matched his deep blue eyes. It would be so perfect for him. She could picture him at the wheel of it.

She forced herself to banish the picture and discussed with Hank when he could find time to come over and help her fit on the canvas top. That settled, Hank went back to his garage and Tory went back to hers, where she started replacing the Pierce's chrome trim.

She had nothing booked that afternoon, though she had a trip to Logan scheduled the following morning, and was already gearing herself to the fact that she must *not* swing by Commonwealth Hospital on the return trip. Chris had made it plain enough that during this Boston stay he wanted no one but Ed Simmons with him.

The day passed. So, finally, did the evening. Tory watched a movie on television three-quarters through, then gave up and went to bed. She didn't know exactly when Chris was going to have the laser treatment. Had he already had it? If so, had it worked? Or would he be having it tomorrow?

It took all the discipline Tory possessed to drive up to Logan Airport on Tuesday morning and then to turn around and head straight for the Cape, without lingering in the Boston area. She was home before eleven o'clock and immediately switched on her answering machine, and was totally frustrated when she found a message from Ed Simmons. He'd left no return number for her but merely said he'd try again later.

All afternoon, Tory worked on the Pierce with one ear cocked for the sound of the telephone. Hank had said he'd leave the garage early and come over so they could attend to the canvas top, and he arrived around four o'clock. She'd turned on the answering machine in case the sound of their tools, at moments, eclipsed the sound of the telephone ringing. A couple of times, she ran upstairs to check the machine. But there were no messages.

Hank left, and Tory thought about pouring herself a glass of wine. But she really didn't want one. She was too tense to eat or drink. And, though with very little more work she could just about finish the Pierce, she knew she was far too edgy to cope with tools or anything else that required much in the way of concentration or dexterity.

Ed called shortly before eight. "Sorry to be so long getting back to you," he apologized. "Chris and I were going over a few things so I stayed till the end of visiting hours."

Ed paused while Tory held her breath. "Everything went perfectly, Tory," he told her then. "The surgeons feel sure the laser worked. They want Chris to keep reasonably quiet for the next few days, and they'll check him carefully. But they're letting him out of the hospital tomorrow."

"You mean he's coming back to the Cape?"

"No, no," Ed said quickly. "We've arranged for a suite at a hotel near the hospital. I'll be staying with him for a while, anyway. I think he'll be back here in a couple of weeks."

Tory noticed that Ed hadn't mentioned the name of the hotel, and she didn't think that was by accident. Chris didn't want her to know where he'd be. The message came loud and clear. He was still stubbornly determined to leave her out of this particular ordeal. She marveled that he'd even let Ed share the experience with him.

She and Ed talked a few minutes longer, then she said, "Thanks for calling, Ed." And she couldn't resist adding, "When you see Chris . . . give him my love."

Wednesday afternoon Tory thought she saw Gus Burke. She was cutting across a road that led past the local golf course when she saw a man walking along the side of the road, his shoulders hunched over. As she passed him, he glanced up briefly, and Tory froze.

She couldn't be positive from one, brief glimpse of him. She couldn't have sworn in a court of law that it was Burke, but she was eighty percent sure.

She turned right on Main Street and was tempted to reverse her directions and drive past the golf course again so she could get another look at the man. But the Caddy was so distinctive, having it reappear that soon was bound to arouse Burke's suspicions—if it was Burke she'd seen.

She quickly attended to some errands she had to do, then drove home and went straight to the phone. She put in a call to Commonwealth Hospital, hoping maybe she could persuade the hospital to give her the name of the hotel Chris had moved into. She wanted the names and whereabouts of the private detectives he'd hired so she could contact them and tell them about the man walking along the rim of the golf course. But the hospital was not about to reveal Christopher Kendall's whereabouts.

After she'd hung up the phone, Tory tried to gather her wits and come to a sensible conclusion about what to do next. She couldn't quite bring herself to call the Chatham police on such slight evidence. Nor would it be a good idea to confide in Hank about this. Hank was great. He and Paula were both great. And she trusted him implicitly about most things.

But, let's face it, Tory told herself, a couple of beers and Hank's apt to decide I need help and then start asking around about Gus Burke. And that kind of inquiry could very well blow the whole thing.

In the end, Tory didn't say anything to anyone. But she wished Chris had given her the picture of Gus Burke instead of relying upon her to memorize it. She only hoped that maybe one or the other of Chris's private detectives had spotted the man she'd seen and at least questioned him. Then if it really was Burke she had seen, by now he should be in custody.

That afternoon, Tory finished the work on the Pierce. When she'd put the last piece of chrome in place, made the last adjustment, she stood back admiring the car, and a wave of sentiment she tried to brand as ridiculous washed over her. She felt as though she should get a bottle of champagne and rechristen the Pierce. She wished Chris were here to share this moment with her....

She wished more than that. For once Tory let her wishes escape freely, let herself fill with them. She wished she and Chris could clink glasses filled with the bubbly stuff and toast the Pierce, and then that they could go upstairs to her room and make love all night long.

* * *

Chatham's newspaper was a weekly, and it came out on Thursday afternoon. The first ad for the Pierce was in the paper, giving Tory's phone number. She was doing a limo job that afternoon, though, so if there were any calls, she missed them. And no one left a message on the machine.

It was raining Friday. Ruth Ferris called and said she had a cold, and would as soon forego her usual Friday morning excursions. Tory didn't have the heart to tell her that people were supposed to pay for last-minute cancellations. They agreed to try again next week.

After lunch, Tory went down to the garage and started to work on the Ford. She was restless, edgy and annoyed at herself for not being in better control. She wondered if maybe by now Ed Simmons had headed back to the Essex boatyard. He hadn't said exactly how long he was planning to stay with Chris.

Would it be absolutely foolish to call the boatyard and see if Ed was there so she could find out how Chris was doing? Ed would understand. She felt sure of that, but she still didn't make the call.

Maybe Monday. Maybe she'd start off next week with a call to Ed, if she hadn't heard from either Chris or Ed in the interim.

Meantime . . .

The rap on the side garage door startled her. She could make out a shadowy shape through the glass panel that covered the upper half of the door, but the silhouette was not a familiar one. Holding a dinging hammer—not with any idea of self-defense but because she'd happened to be using the tool in her work— Tory approached the door and opened it. She found herself face-to-face with Gus Burke.

This time, there was absolutely no mistaking his identity. Though his head was covered with the hood of the black slicker he was wearing, the face looking down at her was the same face she'd seen in the photo Chris had shown her.

Her initial reaction was shock, rather than fear. But then she felt the fear coming on, deep and strong. She desperately fought to keep it from showing either on her face or in her body language as she coolly asked, "Yes?"

"Afternoon, ma'am," Burke said, touching his fingers to the shiny black hood as if it were a hat he was about to doff. He held out the current issue of the Chatham paper. "Saw your ad," he said. "I'm an antique car collector. Mind if I take a look at the Pierce-Arrow?"

He was already looking at the Pierce-Arrow, which was directly within his range of vision. Then without invitation, he walked past Tory to the car and gazed at it admiringly.

"Sure is a beauty," he said.

Tory silently berated herself for not having had the presence of mind to tell him the Pierce was already sold. To at least say something that would have prevented him from coming beyond the threshold of her garage door.

Did he know she was alone in the house? She thought of calling up the stairs, talking as if there were someone in her kitchen, saying to that invisible someone, "It's okay. I'll be up in just a minute." But she doubted if Burke would be fooled by such a ploy.

He was walking around the Pierce, slowly, deliberately, looking it over as carefully as if he really was an antique auto buff.

Tory clutched the dinging hammer a little tighter. She had no illusions about being able to stave off Burke if he suddenly turned on her. He was a big man, big and burly; she could well imagine he had the strength of an ox. Nonetheless, she might have the chance to get in one, solid blow.

"Seems to me that fixed price you state in your ad is kind of on the high side," he said, surveying the Pierce even more closely. "Could you do better? I can pay cash."

He didn't look at her as he spoke, but Tory didn't need to see a shifty expression to be sure he was lying. "I consulted some experts in the field," she said. "They say the price is right. So, no, I wouldn't be inclined to lower it. Especially when my first ad came out only today."

Burke appeared to take her negative reply under serious consideration, then shook his head dolefully. "Too much," he concluded. "You decide to knock off two or three thousand, and we can do business."

He was heading toward the door as he spoke. Tory only hoped he'd keep right on going. Once he was out the door she was going to lock every lock in the place, chain every chain. She didn't want Burke returning here after dark.

On the threshold, he advised, "I'll keep in touch."

Tory merely nodded, waited till he'd gone out the door, then locked it, bolted the chain and made certain the big garage door was securely locked as well. Then she dashed up the stairs, heading toward the dining-room window, which overlooked her side driveway. She peered out from behind the curtains, hoping Burke wouldn't glance in her direction and get a glimpse of her. He didn't.

As she lost him from view, Tory sped to her living-room windows where she could pick him up again. She watched him walk out the driveway into the street, and keep going, heading toward the downtown section of Chatham. Only when he had been out of sight for at least three minutes did she move away from the window...to discover that she was shaking like an aspen in the wind.

She had to get in touch with Ed Simmons. That was her first thought. She went out to the kitchen, consulted the phone directory for Connecticut information and then glanced anxiously at the wall clock. It was nearly four. She could only hope the Essex boatyard didn't close early on Friday afternoons.

The phone was answered on the second ring, but the man at the other end of the line told her, courteously, that Mr. Simmons was out of town, and she was afraid he was going to hang up on her with that. "Wait!" she commanded, and there was no mistaking the urgency of that single word. "I *have* to get in touch with him," she said. "He must have left a number there. If you don't want to give it to me, you can call him yourself and ask him to phone Tory Morgan in Chatham, Massachusetts. This involves Gus Burke, the employee who was fired last fall. He was in my house this afternoon."

It was Chris who called back, not Ed Simmons. "What the hell is happening, Tory?" he asked, his voice taut.

She'd been sitting at the kitchen table for the past fifteen minutes, waiting for the phone to ring. Her nerves were shrieking, and she was on the verge of tears.

"Tory," Chris sounded as unnerved as she felt. "Are you all right?"

"Yes, I'm all right."

"Did you actually tell Tom down at the boatyard that Burke was in your house this afternoon?"

"Yes."

"Have you called the police?"

"No."

Chris swore in a way she'd never heard him swear before, then finished, "For God's sake, why not? I'll get off the phone. You call the cops, then call me back. I'm at the Copley Plaza in Boston."

"No," Tory protested. "No. All right, I'll call the police after we hang up. But first I want to tell you what happened. I...I finished the Pierce the beginning of this week."

"Under other circumstances, I'd say 'Congratulations,'" Chris said dryly.

"There was just time to get an ad in this week's Chatham paper. The paper came out yesterday afternoon. Then around three-fifteen today, or maybe a little later, I was working in the garage and...and..."

Chris's voice was gentle. "Burke came?" he asked.

"Yes. He had the paper with him. He pretended he was interested in buying the Pierce. He really looked the car over."

Chris swore again. "Listen to me, Tory. Now listen to exactly what I'm going to tell you. Ed is on another phone calling the two private detectives we have in Chatham. Their names are Ray Janson and Bill Di-Carlo. They'll have IDs.

"Give one of them the keys to the Pierce and let him get it out of your garage as quickly as possible. I've known the lieutenant on the Chatham Police Force for years. Rod McDougal."

"I've met him," Tory said.

"We were kids together—like Hank and I were. I haven't seen McDougal since I've been back, but I think he'd still consider us friends. I'm going to ask McDougal to find a safe place to stash the Pierce."

"What are you saying?"

"I'm saying that Burke could come back to your place and do the same kind of job on the Pierce that he did on the boats down in Essex."

"But why?"

"Because it would be another way of getting at me." Chris went on, his voice very low, "He must have latched on to some of the local gossip. He must know that you and I have been seeing each other."

"Seeing each other?" Tory nearly laughed out loud. "Chris, the only real date we've had outside our two houses was the night you took me to the Beachside Inn. Other than that, you've been employing me, not dating me."

"Probably being seen at the Beachside Inn was enough," Chris said. "I should have had the sense to take you to dinner somewhere out of town. Anyway... let's assume we were seen, somebody gossiped, Burke heard the gossip. Thus far, he's limited his thoughts about getting revenge on me to vandalism. Your Pierce would be a perfect target. So... go along with me, will you?"

"I can't believe this is happening," Tory muttered.

"I wish I'd never gotten you into it," Chris said bitterly. "Tory, Ed's just told me he's already called the Chatham cops. Just be sure right now that you don't let anyone in without identification unless you know them very well. I'm ninety-nine percent sure Burke's working alone, but I don't want to chance that extra one percent."

"Chris..." Even in the middle of all this turmoil, Tory's thoughts zeroed in on *him*.

"Yes?"

"Are you all right? I mean are you really all right?"

"I'm fine," Chris said brusquely. "Tory, look, I have calls to make. I'll be in touch with you later."

He hung up first. Tory stood, holding the phone receiver, hearing its signal droning in her ear, but it was a while before she hung up.

Twenty minutes later, her front doorbell rang, and she went cold all over. Logic told her Gus Burke wouldn't be apt to come back and walk right up to her front door—not if Chris was right in his suspicion.

A peek out the window told her Lieutenant Rod McDougal was her visitor. She opened the door to the tall, slim, dark-haired man, who had a rather sharp-featured but pleasant face.

"Tory," he greeted her.

"Come in, Rod."

"Have Janson and DiCarlo touched base with you yet?" he asked as she let him into the living room.

"No, you're the first."

"You have no doubt this was Gus Burke who approached you about the car you have for sale, Tory?"

"I'm sure it was him."

"You've met him before?"

"No, Chris Kendall showed me his photograph last weekend," she said.

"I see. You've talked to Chris on the phone, I understand."

"Yes, just a little while ago."

"He called me right after he finished speaking to you. He wants to put this antique auto of yours under wraps. You're in agreement with that?"

"It seems to be the sensible thing to do."

"It is." Rod nodded. "If this man Burke continues to follow the pattern he seems to have established, your car could be next in line. That would be unfortunate. I understand it's a valuable automobile and you've put a lot of hours of restoration work in on it. Now if you'll give me the keys..."

Tory got the keys to the Pierce for Rod, took him down to the underground garage and hoisted open the big door. The door had a tricky mechanism she was familiar with. After a moment of tugging, it opened obediently for her.

"This car *is* a beauty," Rod said, eyeing the Pierce admiringly. "I'll take good care of it. Tory, I came over in a cruiser with Officer Denton. Denton's parked out in front, and he'll stay there until Chris Kendall's two men get here. Okay?"

"Yes," she said, but the idea that she needed protection by the police as well as private investigators suddenly seemed awfully farfetched to her. Wasn't everybody overreacting? On the other hand, it was definitely Gus Burke who had showed up in the garage a while ago, and he hadn't been looking to buy a restored vintage car.

She hesitated, then said, "Rod?"

He was opening the door of the Pierce-Arrow, and he turned. "Yes?"

"Last Wednesday, late morning, I was driving past the Chatham Bars golf course and I saw a man walking along the side of the road. I thought then it was Gus Burke...."

Rod stared at her. "Why didn't you call us?" he demanded.

"I suppose I didn't want to bother the police. I mean…I wasn't absolutely sure it was Burke. I got just one, quick glimpse of his face. But now that I've seen him again, I'm certain it was him. I don't know what good it does to tell you that at this late date…."

"I suppose I'd rather know it now than never," Rod allowed. "If you'd just gone to the nearest phone booth the other day, though, maybe we could have gotten to the scene in time to pick him up. The man vanishes like a ghost in a haunted house. Seems to reappear almost at his own whim. So it would have been a help to be able to pinpoint him to a definite location. If you glimpse him again…"

"You don't have to ask," Tory said, subdued.

At nine o'clock that night, the phone rang. Tory was propped up in bed, trying to read. She'd gone to bed early again because she was incredibly tired; but she was learning that being incredibly tired didn't mean that sleep came easily.

She picked up the receiver, knowing that downstairs in her kitchen, one of Chris's private investigators would be picking it up simultaneously.

"Tory?" Chris asked her. "Are you okay?"

Tory closed her eyes tightly, briefly blotting out everything except the sound of his voice. Then she said, "Yes," and added, "Mr. DiCarlo's on the downstairs phone, Chris."

"You can hang up, Bill," Chris advised good-naturedly. There was a click of the receiver.

"I was the one who suggested that Bill stay at your place tonight," Chris said. "I hope you don't object."

"No, I don't object," Tory said. Bill DiCarlo was a short, olive-complexioned man who looked like somebody's benevolent uncle. "Actually, it's . . . well, it's good to have someone in the house."

"It seemed the wise course to take, just in the event Burke should decide to circle back there tonight," Chris said. "I take it Rod has the car?"

"Yes."

"Tory, this will only be for a day or two," Chris said. "Again, I can't tell you how sorry I am to have gotten you into it. But Burke can't hide out forever. He'll have to surface, and when he does, the police are going to be ready for him. It won't be much longer, Tory."

Chris spoke with a conviction he didn't feel. So far Gus Burke had eluded several law enforcers. But he and Ed had agreed that Burke's picture should be released, shown around Chatham, now that he'd already involved Tory in the act anyway. That would be done tomorrow.

Maybe the picture would do the trick. Maybe it wouldn't. Regardless, Chris had his own plan, and tomorrow he'd be putting it in operation.

The doctors wanted to see him for an occasional checkup, but there was no need for him to stay on in Boston. He'd stayed this long only because he'd hoped that if Gus Burke knew he was in Boston he'd head for Boston himself. Now he'd be leaving in the morning, and he intended to set himself up as a red herring, leaving a trail even the most rank amateur could follow.

He had to lure Gus Burke away from Chatham—and from Tory.

Again, he said, "It won't be much longer, Tory. This time next week all this will be a bad memory."

There was so much more he wanted to say to her, but Chris held back the words. Instead he said good-night as quickly as possible, because there was a limit to his self-control and he yearned to blurt out to Tory how incredibly much he loved her.

Before he could blurt out anything about anything to Tory, though, the matter of Gus Burke had to be resolved. The police officer in Essex had sent a copy of the profile that had been put together on Burke. It showed graphically that Burke was already a dangerous man and could become extremely dangerous if foiled.

That worried Chris. Burke could easily feel foiled by the removal of the Pierce, if the car was next on his sabotage list. Infuriated, he might turn against Tory.

On the other hand, it would have been a terrible thing to have left the car where it was, an open invitation to Burke to get a little more revenge. Tory had worked so long and hard on that car.

Chris went to his hotel window and stared out over Copley Square. It was still drizzling, the wet city streets glistened and some of the people scurrying along were carrying umbrellas. He opened the window, leaned out and felt April's moisture dampen his cheeks. He heard laughter below his room and, looking down, saw a man and a woman just coming out of the hotel. They started down the street and then paused. Then, regardless of passersby, the man took the woman in his arms, and locked in an embrace, they kissed.

Chris had never envied anyone else quite so much.

Chapter Thirteen

Ray Janson showed up at Tory's house at eight o'clock the next morning. Bill DiCarlo had spent the night dozing fitfully on Tory's lumpy living room couch. He'd acceded gratefully to Tory's suggestion that he go upstairs and shower, and by the time he appeared back in the kitchen, Janson was already sitting at the table working on the coffee Tory had brewed.

Janson had red hair, green eyes, freckles; he looked like a middle-aged leprechaun. He grinned at his partner and teased, "Life of Riley."

"So who's complaining?" DiCarlo shot back and accepted a mug of coffee from Tory.

Janson grew serious. "Kendall got in touch," he said.

Tory was immediately alert.

"He's leaving Boston this morning," the detective continued. "Going to Essex, says he wants to take a look around the boatyard for himself. He'll stay with

Simmons while he's in Essex. Probably be there two or three days. Then he's heading for Manhattan, says he needs to put in a few weeks at headquarters there to catch up on all the slack of the past few months.''

A few weeks. Tory's spirits plummeted.

"Also," Janson went on, "Kendall thinks we should start circulating Burke's picture around town, start questioning people about whether they've seen him instead of relying on spotting him ourselves. I think he's right about that. We haven't gotten very far with the sit-back-and-look course of action...so now we go public. Tory, you might take a couple of Burke's pictures, if you would, and pass them out to anyone you know who's in a position to come in contact with a lot of people."

Tory immediately thought of Hank. Melson's was the most popular and successful garage in town, not to mention its key location. Also Hank had lived in this town all his life, he knew a great many people, and he had a very sharp eye.

"I'll be glad to circulate the pictures for you," she told Ray.

"Good." Ray approved. "They're being sent this morning by courier. They were going to fax them, but they thought the reproduction might not be good enough to make an identification. I'll get a couple of copies over to you as soon as they arrive." Ray hesitated, then said, "I don't want to frighten you, Tory, but...take it easy, will you?" His next words almost paraphrased what Chris had told her earlier. "What I'm saying is, be careful what you do, where you go. When you're alone here in the house, keep the chains on the doors, and don't let anyone in unless you know them, or they have identification. We think Burke works alone, but that's something we can't be sure of. He may know someone here in town, be holed up with them. He may be offering a payoff in exchange for some help. Right now, there's no way of knowing.''

Ray went on. ''When you're out, keep in circulation. Stay in places where there are other people. Restaurants, stores, pharmacies, the town library. Matter of fact, I'd rather you'd *stay* out as much as possible, except try to be back here by dark. Either Bill or I will be here with you each night. But until we're actually inside the front door, watch it, will you? There's no telling how paranoid Gus Burke has become at this point.''

At the moment Ray didn't look at all like a middle-aged leprechaun. He looked deadly serious, and Tory nodded, even though what Ray was suggesting was going to throw a wrench in her plans. She'd avoided scheduling any driving engagements today because she wanted to spend time in the garage, working on the Ford. She *needed* to work on the Ford, dammit! On the other hand, she also needed to retain as much of her sanity as she could. And she knew that working in the garage by herself today would freak her out. She'd be constantly imagining Gus Burke's silhouette suddenly looming up behind the glass-paneled door.

''Okay,'' she said, and forced a smile. ''I'll keep my wheels in motion.''

The weather had cleared. The day was bright and sunny. After the detectives left, Tory quickly straightened things up. She couldn't wait to get out of this house she loved so much.

She made Melson's Garage her first stop. Both bays were occupied with cars up on lifts, and Hank Chase was working on the underside of a car parked just outside the first bay. All she could see of him were his long legs.

She waited till he wriggled out, looked up at her, then stood, wiping his grease-stained hands on a dirty rag.

"Well," he greeted. "What brings you here, partner?"

"I got restless," Tory said, which certainly was true enough.

"Had any calls about the Pierce?"

"Not so far." She didn't want to get into the subject of Burke coming to her garage. She only wanted to let Hank look at the man's picture and tell him if he seemed familiar. Also, she didn't want to point out that between the police, Ray and Bill, and Chris calling her, as well, her phone had been so busy last night anyone interested in the Pierce would have had a hard time getting through.

"You'll be getting some responses," Hank said confidently.

"I expect so." She surveyed the cars in the bays, as well as the vehicle Hank had just been working on. "Looks like you have an assembly-line production here," she observed.

"Busy day," Hank agreed.

"Hank...there was something I wanted to talk to you about. Maybe I'd better swing back later, though."

Tory was aware of Hank's light eyes appraising her carefully. Then Hank said, "If you've got something to talk about, we'll talk about it now, Tory."

"Could we use Mr. Melson's office for a minute?"

"Sure," Hank said easily. "He had a dental appointment. He won't be back for at least another hour. Come on. I'll buy you a soda."

Once they were in the small office, Tory sat down on a folding chair and took the envelope with Gus Burke's photo in it out of her handbag. Holding the picture out to Hank, she asked, "Ever seen this man?"

At first Hank looked at her rather than the picture, and he seemed puzzled. Tory could sense some questions being framed, but then Hank's eyes dropped to the photo and he nodded. "Yeah," he said, "I've seen him. Couple of days ago, matter of fact."

Tory hadn't been prepared for such an instant reaction, and she tensed. "Where?" she asked.

"Here," Hank said, his gesture including the gas station in general.

"What was he doing here?"

"He came to gas up his bike."

"What kind of a bike, Hank?"

"He has a big Honda. Super job. He used the self-service pump to gas it up. I noticed the bike because it was so damn dusty. Nice machine, but it looked like he wasn't taking much care of it."

"But you got a good look at his face?"

"Not just then," Hank said. "Fact is, I went to the men's room, and I was coming out just as this guy was about to come in. He'd been wearing a helmet till then. Had a heavy scarf wound around his throat. Dark goggles. Nothing unusual for a bike rider, but you couldn't see much of his face. As he was heading toward the men's room, though, he took off the helmet and the goggles and so I had a good look at him."

"You're sure it's the same man, Hank?"

Hank frowned. "What's this all about, Tory?" he demanded.

"This man's wanted by the police in Connecticut, Hank. The authorities are virtually certain he's responsible for several sabotage incidents down there. He's on a...well, a sort of personal vendetta. Out for revenge..."

"Who's his target?"

"Chris Kendall," Tory said reluctantly.

Hank pursed his lips. "You've been chauffeuring Chris to Boston pretty regularly, haven't you?" he asked her.

"Yes."

"You've been seeing him on the side, as well?"

"I don't much like that 'on the side,' Hank," she warned.

"What I meant was, you've been dating him occasionally?"

"Very occasionally. Hank, to go back to Burke—did he ask any questions about me, or about Chris Kendall?"

"I wouldn't know," Hank said. "I didn't deal with him myself. I just happened to see him as he was gassing up, then later on my way out of the men's room. Like I said, he used the self-service pump." Hank wrinkled his brow. "I'm trying to remember who else was around. Jim Ellis, I think, and this is his day off. Maybe this guy talked to Jim. When Jim comes in tomorrow, I'll ask him."

Tory nodded. "All right. The thing is...well, the Chatham police are working with the Connecticut police on this, and they need all the information they can get. They think this man is dangerous." She decided she'd better level with Hank. "Also, he showed up at my garage the other afternoon," she said, "the day after the first ad for the Pierce came out."

"What are you saying?" Hank demanded.

"This man—his name is Gus Burke, incidentally—may be getting somewhat paranoid," Tory said. "The police think maybe he found out that Chris and I have seen each other a couple of times, which could make me something of a target, too. If not me, something that belongs to me. Like the Pierce."

Hank scowled. "If I'm hearing you right, that paints a different picture, Tory," he said. "Just tell me what I can do to help."

"I'm going to leave his photo with you," Tory said. "Show it around. Ask around. You know a lot of people. Get all the info you can back to me or go straight to Rod McDougal with it. Meantime... the police have taken the Pierce."

"What?"

"They've put the Pierce in safekeeping," Tory said. "Even I don't know where it is."

"And where is Chris Kendall through all this?" Hank asked her.

"He's been in Boston," Tory said without elaborating. "Now he's on his way to his boatyard in Connecticut where this whole problem with Burke began last fall."

Tory stood. "I have to get along," she said. "Anything you find out, be sure to let me know, Hank."

The groundwork had been laid.

"He must have that Honda stashed somewhere around here," Ray Janson said. "My guess is he's holed up in an empty house, a summer place whose owners aren't apt to be around for several more weeks."

Tory shivered. There were so many summer places in Chatham, some of them right around her. It wasn't very pleasant to think of Gus Burke hiding out in one of them.

Rod McDougal said, "Every cop has been instructed to keep his eyes wide open, especially when he's in the vicinity of summer property. But there are hundreds of summer houses in this town, ranging from cottages to mansions. It's a big field to cover."

It was almost nine o'clock. Janson, DiCarlo and McDougal were sitting with Tory around her kitchen table. Tonight, Ray intended to sleep on her living-room couch, and she wasn't protesting. The thought of Burke in the neighborhood, plus the knowledge that he'd been seen in Melson's Garage a couple of days earlier, was sufficiently unnerving to make her glad she was going to have company.

The phone rang. Since she was closest to it, Tory answered it. But she more than expected the summons would be for one of the detectives, or Rod.

Instead Chris asked, "Tory? Are you okay?"

Her pulse began to pound like a dinging hammer. She glanced quickly toward the three men at her kitchen table, but they were absorbed in their own conversation. "Yes," she said, keeping her voice low. "I'm okay. What about you? Where are you?"

"I'm at Ed's place. I'll be here in Essex through Monday. I plan to spend a big chunk of my time at the boatyard. Tuesday morning, I'll be heading for Manhattan. Tory. . . any word about Burke?"

"Hank spotted him at the garage day before yesterday."

"What was he using for wheels?"

"Evidently that same motorcycle he was spotted on in Connecticut. Hank says it's a big Honda."

"Well, at least now we have a make on it." Chris paused. "You wouldn't think a hulk like Burke would be too hard to spot on an oversize bike."

"They don't think he uses the motorcycle that much, Chris. It makes him too conspicuous. They figure he must have come up here from Essex on it, though. There doesn't seem much doubt it's his major transportation."

"Then if he heads out of town on it they should get him."

"There are a lot of roads leading out of town, Chris."

Chris didn't answer that.

Just hearing Tory's voice made him yearn to be with her. He needed her right now. He needed her softness, her warmth, her caring. He wished they could blot out time and problems and concentrate solely on each other. One or the other of them seemed constantly to throw up obstacles in the path of their relationship, and he wondered how many of those obstacles were really valid.

He zeroed back to the present. "Tory," he asked her, "who's with you right now?"

"Ray and Bill and Rod," she said.

"All on a first-name basis, eh?" Chris asked, and tried to tell himself the stab of jealousy he was feeling was totally ridiculous.

"Yes," Tory answered him.

"One of the detectives is going to stay at your place through the night, isn't he?"

"Yes. Ray, tonight."

"Let me speak to him, will you, Tory? But first . . ."

"Yes?"

Chris very nearly said he loved her. Then he got hold of himself and said, instead, "Look, be careful, will you?"

"I'm being careful, Chris."

"Good. Keep it that way."

Saturday night passed, and Sunday morning Tory went downstairs and made coffee for a sleepy-eyed Ray Janson who, like his partner, had discovered that Tory's living room couch had a lot of lumps in it.

Tory had a Sunday trip scheduled to pick up some people who were returning from Florida. It was good to get on the road again. It was a beautiful day. She put the top down on the convertible and let the spring air caress her face. Thinking about Chris at the boatyard in Essex, she felt a pang of fear.

Suppose Gus Burke already had left Chatham and was heading for Essex even now. It seemed to her that Chris was being too casual in announcing his comings and goings and instructing the private investigators to show Burke's picture around openly, and...

Her thoughts tumbled, one over the other, and she was glad when she reached the airport to find that her clients' plane was going to be on time so she'd have no further chance right now to worry and brood.

It was midafternoon when Tory pulled into her driveway and brought the Caddy to a stop in front of the rear garage. Immediately she stiffened.

The garage door was slightly open, and she knew she'd shut it securely when she left that morning.

She'd put the top up on the convertible for the return trip, but after dropping off her clients she'd rolled down all the windows. So she clearly heard all the outdoor sounds: a bird chirping, the leaves rustling in the breeze, the squawk of a seagull soaring overhead. But beyond the sounds of nature, there was nothing but silence. An ominous silence.

Tory glanced at the garage. Could Gus Burke be in there? She glanced toward her house. Could he be *there* waiting for her? She couldn't see beyond the curve of the driveway where it edged around the house to open to the wide ramp that led into the underground garage. He also could be in the underground garage. The door locks weren't all that secure, and Burke was a very strong man.

Her common sense told her that she should back right out of the driveway and head for the police station. On the other hand, she hated to yield to panic.

Forcing herself to take it a step at a time, Tory drove the Caddy around to the back of the house and parked at the edge of the downgrade ramp. The big, main door looked just as it always had. The small side door that led into the garage workshop was closed.

She edged back to the rear garage and positioned the car so that she could get back into it quickly, if need be, and make a speedy takeoff. Then she got out of the car and went over to the slightly opened garage door and pushed it open farther until she had a clear view inside.

As far as she could see, without making a minute inspection, nothing had been disturbed. If she hadn't noticed that the door was slightly opened, she never would have suspected that anyone might have been around in her absence.

Could she have left the door open herself?

Tory shook her head. She was completely disciplined when dealing with the cars and their garaging. She'd no more leave the door of the Caddy's garage open than she would the underground garage door. It was force of habit to close and secure both.

She still wanted the Caddy close enough to make a getaway if she needed to, so she drove around to the front of the house and parked right at the entrance.

Her hands were clammy as she fumbled in her handbag for her house keys. It took raw courage to open the front door. And the minute she stepped inside she *knew* her home had been invaded.

There were no big changes to alert her, just small ones. A chair pushed slightly aside—as if a big man had been impatient to get through her living room. She fancied that she *smelled* Gus Burke in her house, and she shivered. She moved on through the dining room and into the kitchen, and immediately saw the empty beer can on the sink. Burke had helped himself and left the evidence behind, in a gesture of defiance.

Then her eyes fell on the door that opened onto the steps leading down into the underground garage. She'd chained and locked it this morning. Now the chain dangled.

She pushed the switch that would flood the underground garage with light, then stood at the top of the steps peering down. But even before she started the descent, Tory knew that Burke was no longer there. He'd been there, but he'd gone. And he'd left a signature of sorts in the smashed headlights of both the Jag and the Ford. The ball-peen hammer he'd used to do the job was lying on the floor.

Tory could imagine what would have happened if the police hadn't moved the Pierce, and she was shaking as she ran back upstairs and put in a call to Rod McDougal.

* * *

"Obviously," Rod said, "he doesn't give a damn about whether or not he leaves his fingerprints all over the place. I'd say it's equally obvious that he's working alone. I think we can discount the idea that he has a friend or accomplice here in town. Burke has a one-track mind—we can conclude that from everything he's done so far. This is a focused revenge mission he's embarked on. Janson, I think either you or DiCarlo should be here around the clock. I'm going to assign a couple of our guys to an outside watch, but I think one of you should be on the inside."

Ray Janson nodded. "I've called our home base. They're sending up a couple of men who'll take over the outside work Bill and I have been doing. That will free Bill and me to concentrate on this house. But to tell you the truth . . ." Ray hesitated, then grimaced. "I think we're locking the barn door too late," he said.

"You think Burke has already skipped?"

"Possibly. Or else he'll be skipping as soon as he's confident he can make the break without being spotted. I have no doubt he came here today to do a job on the Pierce. He was frustrated when he found the Pierce gone, there's no doubt of that, either. He took out some of the frustration by smashing the headlights on the two cars Tory's working on. Which reminds me—we should all keep a close watch on the Caddy. That's a sabotage job that might interest Burke. Though I'm more inclined to think he may turn his attention away from Tory and head somewhere else."

"Any idea where?" McDougal asked.

"Maybe back to Essex. Maybe he's found out that Kendall's down there. Or he might move on to Manhattan, once Kendall leaves Essex. New York's a big place. It'd be simple for Burke to fade into the crowd down there."

"What would he sabotage in New York, Ray?" Bill DiCarlo asked his partner.

"I think if he goes to New York, he'll be past vandalism or sabotage," Ray said frankly. "I'm no shrink, but I'd say that by that point Burke's frustrations will be eating at him to the point where what he'll want is to get his hands on Kendall, directly."

Tory couldn't listen to this any longer. She and the three men had been sitting around her kitchen table again, but now she got to her feet, unable to be still any longer. "I have a suggestion," she said, facing the men.

"What, Tory?" Rod McDougal asked.

"Bring the Pierce back," she said.

Rod frowned. "Are you saying make the Pierce-Arrow a target for Burke?"

"Yes. Drive the Pierce right down Main Street and all around town, if you like, but make it plain it's heading for home. Put it back in the garage. Dammit, I'll leave the blasted garage door open."

"So Burke can get in and wreck your car, Tory?" Ray Janson asked softly.

"Yes. Better a car than a . . . a human being," Tory said.

Better *anything* than Chris, she was thinking.

Ray Janson's green eyes grew thoughtful. Then he said, "Maybe that's not a bad idea. Maybe you should bring the car back here tomorrow, McDougal. Though, to tell you the truth, I'd give you ninety-to-ten odds against Burke coming here to go after that car again. The man's not an idiot. He's sly, conniving. Clever.

He'll know that from now on we're going to have this place guarded like Fort Knox, so my guess is he won't come near it.

"Like I said before," Ray concluded, "we locked the barn door too late."

Chapter Fourteen

The telephone jangled in the middle of the night, a harsh, discordant noise cutting through the inky stillness. Tory sat bolt upright in bed, her pulse pounding. She reached for the phone on her bedside table and heard Ray Janson exclaim, "The hell you say!"

"It's going up like a torch." Tory recognized Rod McDougal's voice.

What was going up like a torch? Tory switched on the bedside lamp, grabbed her robe and slippers and streaked downstairs.

Ray was just hanging up the receiver on the kitchen wall phone. He met her eyes, and didn't make her pose a question. "The SOB's torched Chris Kendall's garage," he said. "The house would have been next, except the Chatham cops have been keeping an eye on the Kendall place during routine patrols. A cruiser had just swung into the driveway as Burke was making for the house.''

''They got him?''

Ray shook his head. ''They caught him in the beam of their headlights. He took off down the slope back of the Kendall property and made for the woods around the pond. McDougal didn't get into it more than that. They're putting up road blocks, covering the whole area. At some point, he's got to come out.''

''But Chris's garage . . . ?''

''Totaled, McDougal says, or it will be. Our fellow's an accomplished arsonist, damn him.''

''Chris's beautiful Porsche was inside that garage,'' Tory said.

Ray shrugged. ''So Kendall can get himself another Porsche. Thing is, Burke could have made the house his first target. Probably didn't because he had valuable automobiles on his mind. Couldn't get at your Pierce-Arrow, so he went for Kendall's Porsche.

''It would have been a hundred times worse if he'd gone straight for the house,'' Ray pointed out. ''Think of what the stuff in that house must be worth.''

So Kendall can get himself another Porsche.

Unknowingly Ray had said it all in just a few short words. Chris could build himself another garage and buy himself another Porsche and go right on as if nothing had happened. Had it been the Pierce that was torched, Tory would have faced a financial hole that would only get deeper and deeper.

Yet she had willingly offered the Pierce to be used as a lure for Gus Burke, rather than to chance even the slightest risk of Chris being harmed.

Well, *of course* she had offered the Pierce, she thought defiantly. She would have offered it for Chris's sake, for Hank's sake, for anyone's sake.

She turned on her heel and went back upstairs. It took only a few minutes to scrub her face, slip on jeans and a sweater, and tie her hair back in a ponytail. But when she descended the stairs again, the keys to the Caddy in hand, Ray Janson was waiting for her.

"Are you heading where I think you're heading, Tory?" he asked her.

There was no point in denying it. "I'm going over to Chris's place," she said.

"Look," Ray said reasonably, "they're in the middle of dealing with a working fire over there. Fortunately there's not much wind tonight, but they've still got a job to keep the fire from spreading to the house.

"There are plenty of the idly curious on hand, as it is," Ray continued. "Amazing, how many people have police scanners and rush to the scene, regardless of the hour, if they hear any major calls in their vicinity."

"I am not one of the 'idly curious,'" Tory retorted, stung.

"There's no way I can let you out of here by yourself, Tory," Ray said, his tone gentler. "I hope you'll accept that. Kendall would have my hide if I did. But Bill's on his way, he'll stay here to keep an eye on things in case Burke decides to circle back. You can come with me, provided you'll promise me to stick close to either me or Rod McDougal once we're on the scene. I talked to McDougal again while you were upstairs. They still haven't got Burke. It's McDougal, in fact, who suggested he might try to come back here."

The grandfather clock in the living room struck four. "It'll start to get light in another half hour or so," Ray said. "My guess is that Burke will manage to slip by the police net while it's still dark, and then he'll be looking for a place to go. Maybe back to where he's been hiding out, if he can easily reach it. Maybe here . . . if he's planning another case of arson. We can't predict what he's going to do, Tory. I'm no psychologist, as I may have said before, but my hunch is that each time he acts he loses that much more up here." Ray tapped his head. "I'm saying all this because I *want* to scare you," he added. "Don't try for bravado like you did this afternoon, walking into this house by yourself when you didn't know if Burke was in here or not."

She nodded. "Okay, Ray."

He smiled at her. "Honestly okay? You'll go along with me?"

"Yes, I'll go along with you."

A few minutes later, she and Ray started out in his conventional, dark blue, unobtrusive sedan. Ray was tight-lipped. She knew that he would much rather have left her behind, though from the discussion he and Bill had had about the possibility of Burke choosing her house, or the Caddy, as his next target, her home didn't exactly seem the safest haven at the moment, either.

Chris's driveway was choked with fire engines, police cruisers and unmarked cars that probably belonged to some of the volunteer firefighters, or maybe members of the local press. A fire at the Kendall mansion, after all, was no ordinary blaze.

Ray was stopped by a police officer, showed an ID and then was able to park as close to the scene as possible. As she trudged by his side up Chris's driveway, Tory almost wished she hadn't come. Flames still shot skyward through the roof of the impressive, three-car garage, but the building itself already was a skeleton structure. Doomed.

As Ray had predicted, there were a fair cluster of people gathered as close to the blaze as the police would let them get. Ray led Tory past the small crowd, and they saw Rod McDougal talking to the Chatham fire chief.

Rod scowled when he saw Tory, and Ray said hastily, "She wanted to come, McDougal, and as far as I'm concerned it's six of one and half a dozen of another where her safety is concerned. If Burke goes back to her house..."

"Okay," Rod said. "Tory, for God's sake don't go wandering off, though. Stick with Ray or with me."

"She's already been through that drill," Ray stated.

Tory barely heard either of them.

From where she stood, the crowd was to her left, and by turning her head only slightly she could see faces glowing in the reflection of the flames and the emergency lights set up around the scene by the fire department.

In particular she saw one face. Fortunately he was not looking at her. Rather, he was gazing raptly at the flames.

Gus Burke had not only slipped by the police in the darkness, but instead of making a run for it he'd had the colossal gall to return to the scene of his latest crime.

Tory quickly averted her gaze, and in a telltale instant her eyes met Rod McDougal's.

"What is it?" McDougal asked sharply.

"Don't look," Tory urged. "Hear me out first. He's there, in the crowd. That big man, toward the center. He has a gray watch cap pulled down over his head, and he's wearing glasses, but it's Burke."

"Okay," McDougal said, "don't even glance toward him again, Tory. Concentrate on the fire. That's what most people are doing. Fred," he addressed the fire chief, "you and I are going to walk back toward the ladder truck...no hurry, we're going to walk like we would if you wanted to check on something but weren't in a rush. Ray, take Tory and move closer to the house. Casually like you're only interested in a better view. Then get her out of sight as soon as you possibly can."

McDougal concluded grimly, "This time, Burke's not going to get away."

Gus Burke didn't get away. From the vantage point to which Ray led her, Tory saw the Chatham police close in on him. Heard the threats, the verbal abuse with which Burke laced the air as he was being led away.

As the police cruiser's siren wailed through the night, all Tory could think of was that Burke was about to be put behind bars and so finally, finally, Chris would be safe. But instead of that knowledge calming her down, her nerves started to shatter. She began to shake. "Come on, we're getting you home," Ray said, putting an arm around her in a fatherly fashion.

Once in his car, she started to cry, and for a few minutes she thought she was never going to be able to stop. Ray proffered a big white cotton handkerchief. "It's a normal reaction, Tory. You've been under a hell of a lot of strain. It's over, now. Just get that through your head. It's over."

She gained a second father once she got home. Bill DiCarlo insisted on fixing her hot milk laced with bourbon. She didn't think she could down it, but she didn't want to hurt Bill's feelings, so she managed to drink most of it. But then when Bill and Ray suggested she go back to bed, she suddenly didn't want to be alone.

"Okay," Bill compromised. "Curl up on the living-room couch and maybe you'll nod off. Ray and I will both be around. We've got some phoning to do, some notes to make for reports we'll have to write. If you need us, we'll be right in the kitchen."

Tory smiled at Bill gratefully. Ray and Bill were nice men, very nice men. As she followed Bill's instructions, lying down on the living-room couch and spreading an afghan over herself, she was glad that they were both so close at hand. It wasn't until she had seen Burke's contorted face as the police zeroed in on him, and then heard his crazed, verbal abuse, that she'd realized just how dangerous he really was.

Tory awakened to the sound of rain slashing against the living-room windowpanes. A dull gray light filtered through the room. She stretched, and acknowledged that one of these days she'd have to get a new couch. Poor Ray, poor Bill, she thought, trying to sleep on this torture bed.

Then she heard voices coming from her kitchen. Ray's voice, Bill's voice... and another voice.

Tory got up and slowly, hesitantly, made her way to the kitchen door. Across the room, her eyes met Chris Kendall's clear, deep blue gaze.

She stood very still, wanting to move, wanting to rush across the room and fling herself into Chris's arms. Yet she was unable to take as much as a single step.

She supposed she might have known Chris would be notified and would come to Chatham, but she'd been so exhausted earlier that the thought just hadn't occurred to her. Now she wished Ray or Bill had told her

Chris was on the way. Then maybe she'd have been better prepared to face him.

As it was, she had the awful impression that she was looking at a stranger. Maybe because there was no real recognition on his face. She might as well have been someone he'd never seen before, for all the emotion he was showing.

"Hello, Tory." His voice was calm, even.

"Hello," she managed.

"You still look done in." It was Bill DiCarlo, rather than Chris, who was evidencing concern for her.

"I'm okay," Tory said. As she spoke, she was aware that she must look like hell. Her hair was scraggling around her neck. She knew there were deep, dark circles of fatigue under her eyes. Her clothes were rumpled. In contrast, Chris was freshly shaved, and wearing dark blue slacks and a white pullover. He looked clear-eyed, completely in control.

"I made a fresh pot of coffee," Ray said. "How about a cup?"

Coffee. Tory felt as if she'd had so much coffee these past few days she must be drowning in caffeine. "No, thanks," she said. When Ray pulled out a chair at the kitchen table for her she went over and sat down.

"We were just filling Mr. Kendall in on what's gone down," Ray said. "He came here directly from Chatham Airport."

"You got a plane into Chatham Airport at this hour of the morning?" Tory asked incredulously. The kitchen clock told her it was not quite eight o'clock.

"We keep a company plane in Essex," Chris said. "I used it."

"I've always wished I'd gone for a pilot's license," Bill DiCarlo said.

Chris smiled. "It's never too late."

"For me it is."

"I don't know about that, Bill. I only got my license a few years ago."

Bill DiCarlo grinned. "You're a lot younger than I am, Mr. Kendall."

Tory, taking in this conversation, stared at Chris. "*You* flew up here?" she asked him.

He nodded. "Yes."

She didn't know why she should be so surprised to learn that he could pilot a plane. It was just another one of the many things about him she didn't know, she told herself. She and Chris had met under such unusual circumstances. For a while there, she'd literally been in the driver's seat, but even when he was relying on her for transportation she'd never made the mistake of thinking that Chris Kendall was in any sense of the word a dependent person.

No, he stood alone, strong, capable, self-assured. Maybe he'd needed her to chauffeur him around for a while, but now his life was straightened out and whatever need there had been was part of a past that couldn't be restored.

Tory turned to Ray and asked, "Do you suppose I could have that cup of coffee after all?"

Chris watched Ray Janson hand Tory a mug of coffee, watched Tory spoon some sugar into it and noted that her hand was trembling slightly.

She looked totally bushed. He wondered if she'd been out in the fresh air and sunshine at all, lately. She was as white as a sheet.

Probably, he thought grimly, she'd been spending all her free time in her downstairs garage, working over the two cars Hank Chase had found for her. Or else she'd been behind the wheel of the Caddy, driving back and forth to Boston. Trying like hell to make extra money so she could have a new roof put on this house, make her increased mortgage payments and attend to a few other things.

He remembered her reaction when he'd suggested he advance her some funds. He was not about to make that mistake again! Tory was the most flagrantly independent person he'd ever met. Too much pride, too much stubbornness...

Trouble was, he possessed a fair share of those qualities himself.

He was too proud, sometimes too stubborn. His reasons were different from Tory's, but the results were very much the same. They were two strong-willed, blockheaded individuals who'd been hurt in different ways—but again, the results were much the same. They didn't yield easily, either of them.

Chris wondered if the word *compromise* was in Tory's vocabulary.

She was concentrating on the mug of coffee as if it were the only object in the world. Ray Janson and Bill DiCarlo were going over some notes they'd been making, because they wanted to dovetail a couple of the things they had to tell him. Chris, for the moment, had the chance to be unobserved himself as he observed Tory. And he wondered how his heart could possibly hold all the love he felt for her.

When he'd looked up to see her standing in the kitchen doorway it had taken all of his willpower not to cover the space between them and take her in his arms. He'd wanted to sweep her up and carry her upstairs to her bedroom and then to stay with her—not to make love, not then, but just to be with her while she slept for a while.

Instead he'd greeted her as coolly as he would have a virtual stranger. And when he'd seen the hurt on her face, he had briefly despised himself for responding so instinctively to years and years of a set behavorial pattern, instead of striking out on his own.

His father had been deeply in love with his mother; he'd never doubted that. In fact, it had been unassuaged grief that had led his father into the arms of the unscrupulous woman who had stripped him not only of a great deal of money, but of his honor and even his dignity.

Yet for all of the genuine love between his parents, Chris couldn't remember ever seeing them embrace each other in front of him.

Love between his parents—and whatever other strong emotions they'd shared over the years—had gone on beyond closed doors. Once out of the bedroom they had been unfailingly polite and courteous to each other, but there had been no overt affection. Evidently that was the way they'd been brought up, and it was the lesson they'd taught him. Even when his mother died, his father had mourned for his wife behind closed doors. Publicly he had been the same genteel but unapproachable person he'd always been.

Only after his second wife deserted him had Lionel Kendall ever given an indication of the way he really felt. Before he died, he'd broken down in tears and told Chris what a damned fool he'd been....

But that had been very late in the day, Chris thought bitterly.

From an early age, Chris had been conditioned to keep his emotions in. And when he saw Tory standing in the doorway he'd bottled up his feelings, conscious of the presence of Ray Janson and Bill DiCarlo. He'd assumed that Tory would be as embarrassed as his mother might have been if he'd covered the kitchen in two giant steps and clutched her the way he wanted to clutch her and kissed her with a kiss that went straight to the soul.

Would she have been embarrassed?

Maybe, Chris conceded. But maybe the embarrassment would have faded and then the two of them could have faced Janson and DiCarlo—or anyone else who happened to come around—their arms around each other, secure in the knowledge of their mutual love.

Mutual love?

Did Tory love him?

Chris still wasn't sure. At first he'd feared that her responses could be put down to pity, because of his eye problem. She had a big, big heart, Tory did—it hadn't taken much acumen to see that. She was generous and caring. She'd help anyone who needed help. And, yes, there'd been a flow of something very special between them, right from the beginning, insofar as physical awareness of each other was concerned. But that was sexual, and the kind of love he was thinking about included the physical, needless to say, but went way beyond it....

Tory looked up at that instant, and again their eyes met. Chris didn't have time to put his guard up, and he felt Tory must see the way he felt for her written all over his face. But if she did, she wasn't sending out any return messages. Her beautiful, tired face was totally blank.

* * *

The house seemed very empty without Ray Janson or Bill DiCarlo or Rod McDougal around—or Chris.

Tory moved from room to room, knowing that she should get out the vacuum cleaner and some dust rags and furniture polish and make the place shine a little. But she was still too tired to do more than think about what needed to be done.

Even more urgent, she reminded herself, was the need to get down to the garage and work on the Ford so that she could get it finished and put it up for sale. Which reminded her that Rod McDougal would be bringing the Pierce-Arrow back this afternoon, and she'd probably better put a second set of ads in the papers.

Chris had left with Ray and Bill to go to the fire scene. It was a gray day, the sky loaded with heavy, swollen clouds. Maybe it would rain later. She hoped it would. Anything was better than this stillness. But it was an awful kind of day, she thought, for Chris to have to view the remains of his garage, which by now must be little more than a charred ruin.

She shuddered. When she was a child, a house down the block from her parents' home in a Boston suburb had burned and a little girl she knew had been killed in the blaze. Ever since, the sight of a burned-out building had held a special kind of horror for her.

Tory blocked out grim memories and made up her mind that, tired or not, she needed some action.

Housecleaning or car restoring? She felt she should toss a coin, but the answer was fairly obvious. Housecleaning was something that had to be done, granted. And it did give one a sense of satisfaction once it was accomplished. Working on a car, on the other hand, was a kind of therapy for her. And right now she needed all the therapy she could get.

An hour later, she realized she'd made a mistake. She was using a chisel pick hammer on some sharp corners around the moldings on the Ford and her thumb got in the way.

As pain bolted through her, she grabbed a clean rag and wrapped it around the thumb, which was already dripping blood. Upstairs in the kitchen she turned on the cold water tap and stuck her injured finger under the running water. The pain intensified, then settled down into a throbbing, steady mass of misery.

She was still letting the cold water run over her thumb when the phone rang, and at first she ignored the insistent summons. But whomever it was wasn't about to hang up easily. Tory tore off some paper towels, wrapped them around her thumb and picked up the phone receiver.

"I must have gotten you up from the garage," Chris Kendall said.

She hadn't expected to hear his voice. She hadn't known what to expect—hadn't expected much of anything, actually—when Chris walked out of her house with Ray Janson and Bill DiCarlo.

The pain in her thumb was excruciating. Normally she was so extremely careful when she was working on a car that she'd sustained very few injuries. But there'd been a couple of earlier ones, enough to make her know that for a time the thumb was going to keep on hurting more, rather than less.

She fought a bout of giddiness as she said, "I was already in the kitchen."

"What's wrong, Tory?" The question came fast; she wasn't prepared for it.

"N-nothing," she stammered.

"Tory," Chris said, spacing out the words with poorly restrained importance, "what . . . is . . . wrong?"

"I banged my thumb with a hammer, that's all."

"Is it bad?"

"I don't know. I was just washing it off—"

"I'll be right over," Chris said.

Tory was seated at the kitchen table, her hand wrapped in a wad of paper towels, when Chris walked in. Blood was seeping through a corner of the towels.

Chris gently unwrapped the towels, took one look, and said, "You need help with this."

"Don't be ridiculous." She tried to snap out the words, but she didn't have the strength. Fatigue, pain, were taking their toll. All she wanted to do was sit here at the kitchen table without making so much as a move.

But Chris wasn't buying that. Within minutes, he had her out in the car—he'd borrowed Ray Janson's car, she noticed—and within minutes after that Tory was receiving emergency medical treatment.

When she emerged from the treatment room—her hand swathed in an impressive bandage, and a protective shield over the injured thumb—Chris was waiting. She saw the anxiety on his face—it had been all the doctor on duty at the clinic could do to keep him out of the treatment room—and she wondered vaguely why sometimes he seemed to care so much about her and sometimes he didn't seem to care at all.

He took her by the arm and asked, "Did they give you a painkiller?"

"Yep." She'd been given a shot, and she was already beginning to feel a little hazy.

"Need to get a prescription filled?"

"No. The doctor gave me some pain pills."

"Maybe you'd better turn them over to me."

They were standing by Ray's car at the curb when Chris said this, and Tory turned on him defiantly. "Why should I do that?"

"Because you're already sort of groggy, I want to make sure you take the dosage at proper intervals, that's all."

"I'm not about to overdose, if that's what you mean."

"No," he agreed, "I'm sure you wouldn't, deliberately. Now come on. Get in. I'm taking you home."

At the clinic they'd made sure that she had someone to drive her home before they'd release her, and Tory could see why. She was glad of Chris's guiding arm as he led her into her house, and she collapsed on a chair right inside the living room door.

"That must have been quite a whopper they gave you," Chris said, surveying her.

Tory shook her head. "I've never had much medication," she confessed. "I think I have a stronger reaction than a lot of people, that's all."

Chris looked worried. "We'll get you upstairs and into bed. Regardless of the thumb, you look like you could use about twenty-four hours of straight sleep."

His arm, holding her tightly, felt warm and wonderful as he led her up the stairs. Tory expected that once he got her as far as her bedroom, he'd leave. But he didn't.

"Where can I find a nightgown?" he asked her.

"Chris," she began to protest, "look, I can—"

"Tory, where do I find a nightgown?"

"Second dresser drawer," she said, then gave way to what nature was telling her to do and stretched out on the bed, nestling her head against the pillows.

Chris began to undress her, and she couldn't deny that she loved the touch of his hands on her body. She obeyed his instructions, lifting her shoulders up a little as he unhooked her bra, raising her hips as he slipped off her skimpy, pink satin, lace-trimmed briefs. She loved pretty lingerie. It was one of the very few extravagances she permitted herself. Also, she took good care of her finery. She'd had the pale blue silk nightgown Chris was slipping over her head for a long time, but it was as lovely as it had been when it was new.

Chris smoothed the sleek fabric over her hips. His hands lingered, and she could feel the warmth of his palms seeping into her thighs. Desire was there, all right, but it was a sort of vicarious desire right now, like something standing off in the wings rather than taking center stage. She wanted Chris next to her forever. She wanted his hands on her forever. She wanted *him* forever. But right now she didn't have the strength to express any of that.

Tory cuddled down in her bed and fell asleep.

Chris sat down in the old Salem rocker next to Tory's bedroom window, and watched her sleep. As the afternoon lengthened, he went downstairs once, made himself a peanut-butter sandwich and took it and a glass of milk back to Tory's room, sipping and munching as she continued to sleep.

It seemed to him that the fatigue previously etched on her lovely face was gradually easing. As she slept, she looked softer and softer, and so very young and vulnerable. Love and tenderness overflowed in Chris as he watched her, but there was also some resentment mixed in.

If she hadn't been so damned tired, she would never have done that job on her thumb. He was certain of that. He'd seen Tory work. He knew how meticulous she was, how careful. But today she'd been exhausted when she dragged herself down to her garage, or the accident would never have happened. Most similar mishaps in his boatyards occurred only when employees weren't up to par—either physically or emotionally.

He didn't want her working this way. The way she had her life planned out right now, most of the time she'd either be driving for hire or working until God knows how late in her garage.

He respected what she did, admired her skill. But working two full-time jobs until you were ready to drop was no life for a beautiful, twenty-eight-year-old woman. Especially when it didn't *have* to be this way.

Chris looked at Tory, saw the even rise and fall of her breasts, and marveled that he'd been able to restrain himself while undressing her. It would have been so easy to yield to his own needs, to slip down onto the bed by her side and to take her. But he didn't want to "take" Tory. Anything between them had to be mutual, give-and-take—in equal measures.

The problem with Tory was that she was all too willing to give, but much too reluctant to take anything back in return.

Chris scowled. He didn't know what he was going to do about this complex, wonderful woman he'd fallen in love with. But, by God, he was going to have to do something!

Chapter Fifteen

I've got a buyer for the Pierce, Tory," Hank Chase exulted.

Tory had stopped by Melson's Garage to gas up the Caddy, and the minute he saw her, Hank dashed over, a smile creasing his face. "I was just trying to get you on the phone," he said. "This is a sure sale. No haggle about the price. The guy really wants the car."

"That's wonderful, Hank," Tory said. And it was, even though it made her feel very sad to think of losing the Pierce. It was never easy to give up a car she restored, but with the Pierce it was going to be especially rough because she wished so much she could afford to give this marvelous classic automobile to Chris.

She looked up at Hank. "Who's the buyer?" she asked. "When does he want the car? I thought I might give her one additional waxing."

"She already shines like a star," Hank said. "You don't need to do another thing to her, Tory, except maybe dust her off. She probably picked up a little dust when Rod McDougal was driving her back and forth from your place."

"I guess you're right," Tory agreed reluctantly. "Who's the buyer?" she asked again. "Does he want the car immediately? Where do we have to deliver it?"

"He's sending a representative to Chatham to pick up the Pierce," Hank said.

"Sending a representative? To whom are we selling? Some Near Eastern potentate?"

"No," Hank said. "The client is well-known, though. For that reason he prefers to remain anonymous."

"Driving around in the Pierce-Arrow isn't exactly going to preserve his anonymity," Tory said. "That's a pretty conspicuous car."

"I don't think he intends to drive it, Tory."

Tory frowned. "Then what does he intend to do with it?"

"He's building an auto museum on his estate," Hank said, "for his own pleasure. It'll be open to friends, but not to the public."

"Where's his estate?"

"Somewhere up on the North Shore," Hank said vaguely.

"You mean he's *never* going to drive the Pierce?"

"That's the way I understand it."

"I can't say that makes me happy," Tory grumbled. "That car cries to be driven. She's a beautiful, elegant lady. She shouldn't be kept hidden away, just for the pleasure of some rich man who probably won't even fully appreciate her in the first place."

Tory signed the chit the gas pump attendant handed her, then turned back to Hank to say, "We have to talk about this, Hank."

"Tory," Hank said, perplexed, "I can't figure out where you're coming from. Before the ads even come out in the papers again, I get this chance to sell the Pierce for you, and you're acting like I put coal in your Christmas stocking."

"No," Tory said absently, "it's not that."

"Then what is it?"

"Something," she said. "I'm not sure what. Look, Hank, I have some errands to do. I'll get back to you later. Or maybe you could come over when you're through? I'll be working down in the garage."

He nodded. "Okay."

Before Tory had driven three miles, though, she turned the Caddy around and headed back to Melson's Garage. Hank was in the second bay, wiping his hands off on a grease rag.

Tory approached him and said without preamble, "I think I've figured this out."

Hank continued wiping his hands, even though he'd gotten most of the grease off them. "Figured what out?" he asked her.

"Chris Kendall's the one who's made an offer for the Pierce, right?"

Hank blinked, then tried to look so guileless Tory would have burst out laughing, if she hadn't been so furious.

"Tory..." Hank began.

"Hank, don't bother," Tory said. "You have an absolutely transparent face, for one thing, and you're the worst liar in the world, for another. I'm asking you straight. It *is* Chris Kendall who made the offer, isn't it?''

"Yes," Hank muttered unhappily.

"And the two of you cooked up all this camou-flage—North Shore millionaire, antique auto museum, the whole phony setup . . ."

"Tory, it wasn't a case of cooking anything up . . ."

"Then why didn't you simply tell me that Chris wants to buy the Pierce? Or why didn't Chris pick up the phone and make the offer himself?''

Hank sat down on an upturned wooden crate. "Because he didn't think you'd sell to him," he said.

"He knows damned well I wouldn't sell to him," Tory snapped.

Hank sighed. "Okay," he said. "Okay. Maybe this is none of my business, which is what you'll probably tell me. But I don't understand what's going down here. Chris wants the car, and he certainly has the money to buy it. You need to sell the car, because you need cash. We both know that. So I'm damned if I see what the problem is.''

"Chris isn't making the offer because he wants the Pierce," Tory said flatly. "Oh, I know he admires the car. Maybe he'd even like to own it. But that's not the real reason why he's doing this.''

"I'm not following you," Hank admitted. "The guy's offering to pay the price you're asking. Would he do that if he didn't want the car?''

"Yes," Tory said. "Don't ask me to explain, but yes, he'd do that. Look, Hank, I'm sorry to renege on your deal, especially since there's a ten-percent commission in it for you if you originate the sale.''

"I wasn't thinking of the commission, Tory."

"I know you weren't. Nevertheless... I'm sorry. But once the ads are out, another buyer will show up. Maybe we'll have to dicker with the price a little, but we can handle that. Meantime..."

"Yes?"

"Meantime," Tory said, "get back to Chris Kendall and tell him the Pierce is not for sale."

Tory did her errands, went home and thought about dropping everything and trying to find something to watch on TV. Her thumb hurt. She still felt tired. And a dull anger surged deep inside when she thought about Chris's attempt to perform an act of charity by buying the Pierce.

Didn't he know she didn't want financial help from him? Didn't he know that the only thing she wanted from him, the only thing she'd ever want from him, was love?

Tory made herself a cup of tea, took it into the living room and flicked through the channels on the television set. Finding nothing that intrigued her enough to hold her attention, she changed into her work jeans, slipped on an old, red sweater and went down to the garage.

She'd ordered headlight replacements for both the Ford and the Jag, but now the gaping holes where the headlights had been reminded her of Gus Burke, and she shuddered. She knew the Connecticut police had made the trip to Chatham and taken him back with them. What worried her was that there was always a chance he could go free.

She set to work. With her left hand bound the way it was, her thumb sticking out stiffly with a protector over it, handling tools wasn't easy. She had to proceed slowly and carefully, and she was beginning to realize that with her acquired handicap even getting the Ford in shape was going to take a lot longer than she'd anticipated, to say nothing of the Jag. It would be a while before her thumb was back to normal again.

Well . . . she could only do what she could do.

Bent on accomplishing that much, anyway, Tory was so startled when she heard a sound at the side garage door that she dropped the hammer she was holding, nearly hitting her foot.

She glanced toward the door, and froze. She saw the bulky shape of a man in back of the glass panel, and all she could think was that Gus Burke had somehow gotten out of jail and come back here.

Then she got hold of herself. It couldn't be Burke. Common sense told her it couldn't be Burke. Nevertheless, she picked up the fallen hammer, and clutching it firmly started toward the door.

Chris Kendall stood on the threshold.

He looked at her, took in the way she was clutching the hammer and said, "My God, I frightened you."

He advanced into the garage, watching her closely. "You thought Burke might have come back, didn't you?"

"It was just a crazy idea, just for a second," Tory said defensively. "Once I really stopped to think . . ."

"You don't have to apologize," Chris said. "It's a logical reaction. For the record, though, Burke's not going to be around again, Tory. Right now, they've sent him to a state facility for thirty days, where he'll undergo psychiatric evaluation. That'll determine whether or not he's competent to stand trial. One way or the other, he's not going to be turned loose on society unless—until—that warped brain of his can be straightened out. If he does stand trial, the cops have plenty of evidence to make the case against him stick.

"The police discovered, incidentally, that Burke was hiding out in a cottage on the Bailey property, which is only about a quarter of a mile from my place. Their main house has a security system, but the cottage doesn't. Also, Burke has admitted he was watching my place. He saw us the night we came back from the Beachside Inn. After that, it was relatively easy for him to track down the Caddy and find out who you were."

Chris was moving toward the Ford as he spoke. "Nice car," he commented. "I can see the potential. But *four* flat tires?"

"Tires don't hold up for thirty years when a car's sitting in a garage," Tory said rather stiffly. "I have new tires on order. I deal with a company that specializes in tires for vintage automobiles."

Chris nodded, then looked at the empty holes where the headlights should have been. "I wish I'd had the satisfaction of getting my hands on Gus Burke for just a little while," he said bitterly. "What a rotten thing to do to you."

"It will take a bit longer to restore the Jag, that's all."

"Do you accept everything so easily?"

"I don't know what you mean."

"If I were you, I'd be mad as hell at what Burke did to the Jag. I'm certainly mad as hell at what he did to my garage, and *my* car. That awful, charred smoke smell has even filtered into the house."

Chris looked around, then said, "Much as I like your garage, it isn't the best place to talk. Could we go upstairs, Tory?"

She knew what he was going to get into. Hank had told him she refused to sell the Pierce to him. He'd come here to take that up with her. But it was a subject she didn't want to discuss with him.

"I really can't spare the time right now, Chris. I'm way behind on my work, as it is. I need to put in a few more hours before I call it quits."

"You're beginning to sound like a workaholic."

"I need to work," she said defensively.

"And I don't, is that it?"

She stiffened, "That wasn't meant as a personal remark."

"Wasn't it? For the record, Victoria Morgan, let me tell you that I work extremely hard, and have for most of my life. You happened to meet me in my idle time. Enforced idleness, I might add. I didn't choose it. But under normal circumstances I think I could match you with the job hours I put in. It's only recently that I've come to realize that maybe I'm doing myself an injustice, that maybe there is more to life. But that's another story."

Chris folded his arms, and surveyed her. He was wearing a dark blue parka, his hair was slightly wind tousled, and he could do with a shave. Right now he projected quite a different image than that of the man she'd driven to the Boston hospital complex on those four occasions.

On the other hand, this was not the first time Tory had seen the "other side" of Chris Kendall. Nor the first time she'd wondered which was the "real" Chris— the cool, perfectly groomed business executive, or this far more approachable man who was looking at her with a dangerous spark in those deep blue eyes.

"Why did you refuse to sell me the Pierce?" he demanded.

He had a way of throwing questions at her when she wasn't ready for them. Tory's chin tilted up instinctively, her jaw tightened. "I think you know why," she said.

"Because you thought I was trying to dole the money to you out of a sense of pity, is that it?" he asked. And, before she could answer, added, "If that is the answer, maybe you can appreciate how I felt that night my sight went and you seemed so damned willing to make love. I felt like I was being washed all over by your pity."

"Then you were wrong," Tory snapped.

Chris smiled. "You mean you wanted to make love to me?" he asked lazily. "You really wanted to make love? You didn't just feel sorry for me?"

Tory wanted to throttle him. How could he *tease* about something like that?

Chris moved closer and she drew back, but in drawing back she came up against the hood of the Ford and could go no farther. He reached for her and tugged her toward him; with one hand damaged and the other still holding a hammer there wasn't much she could do about resisting his embrace.

His mouth closed on hers, and she began to drown in the intense sweetness of his kiss. There was no way she could refuse his invitation, no way that she could refrain from kissing him back. The hammer dropped to the ground, and she let it go. She nestled her head against Chris's chest, and wished she had the willpower to pull away from him.

"I just realized something about garages," he said thickly.

"What?"

"There's no place in them to make love. Unless you go for making love in the back seat of a car."

Tory had to laugh, and her laugh snapped the tension she was feeling. But it also set loose an incredibly strong surge of desire. Dear God, but she wanted Chris now and forever. But she couldn't have him now and forever. She moaned softly, and he heard her.

"What is it?" he asked, leaning toward her anxiously. "I didn't bang into your thumb, did I?"

"No."

"Tory, what is it?" He was searching her face, and she was afraid of what he might see written there. If he knew how much she loved him, how much she wanted him, her last defense would be wiped out like a sand castle being destroyed by a rising tide. She had to hang on to her pride, dammit. . . .

"Let's go upstairs," Chris said abruptly.

Tory went along with that, but once upstairs she turned into the living room. She was not about to take the second flight with him right now. Not about to go into her bedroom with him, with consequences that would be absolutely inevitable.

Chris, however, made no move toward the second flight of stairs. He sat down in an armchair, thrust his legs out in front of him and clasped his hands together. "We need to straighten out some things between us, Tory," he said.

"What is there to straighten out?"

"Quite a bit, I'd say. First priority, you're going to have to make an attempt to get rid of some of the preconceived ideas you have about me. I'm not the playboy you seem to think I am, and I'm not a dilettante."

"I never accused you of being either."

"No. But whereas in the eyes of the law you're supposed to be considered innocent until proven guilty, I've often felt it's just the opposite with you where I'm concerned. I've felt I have to prove my innocence. It's difficult to get very far in a relationship when you're always having to make your own case."

She didn't answer.

"What you fail to realize—or even to contemplate—is that you and I are not so very different, Tory."

"How can you say that?"

"Because it's true. We're both pigheaded. . . ."

She stared at him.

"We both have hang-ups because of things that happened in the past. In my case, a lot of the way I've felt about women stems from a job a certain woman did on my father, a couple of years after my mother died. My father was very lonely. A much younger woman took advantage of that fact, married him, and then as much as told him to go to hell, divorced him, and got an outrageous financial settlement out of him. My father was never the same. Neither was I. I thought to myself, 'I'll be damned if any woman is ever going to do that to me,' and I've seen to it that no woman has ever come close to doing it to me. And now, as it happens, the woman I love has no use for my inheritance anyway. . . ."

Tory was sure her pulse skipped several beats.

"Don't you know I love you, Tory?" Chris asked gently. "It seems to me you should. You're a very perceptive person. I would think you would have felt it in our lovemaking that night at my house. And not just then. I think maybe I've shown my love for you even more those times when I *haven't* made love to you, like the other night. Do you think it was easy to undress you and look at that gorgeous body of yours and want you the way I wanted you . . . and then go sit in a rocking chair and watch my sleeping beauty sleep?"

She couldn't answer him.

"Ray Janson told me you offered to have the Pierce-Arrow brought back here as a lure to Gus Burke, to get him off my trail," Chris said softly. "I think that said it all to me—even though it's beginning to seem that you won't say a damned thing yourself." Chris paused. "I'd like to know how you feel about me, Tory."

Tory lowered her eyes, stared at her bandaged thumb. "I don't know," she said.

"You don't *know*?" Chris echoed.

"I can't honestly believe that we belong together," she said. "And I don't agree with you that we're ... not all that different. I don't see how we could be anything but very different...."

Chris chuckled. "Oh, we're different enough to make it interesting," he acknowledged. "But what you're talking about is surface stuff, Tory, and I'm delving deep."

"I can't see how we could ever fit into each other's lives," she said, and then wished she hadn't said it. Chris, for all he'd been talking about, hadn't said anything about her sharing his life with him.

"No one simply fits into anyone else's life," Chris said. "That's storybook stuff. In the real world, you have to make adjustments. I would think you'd have learned that in dealing with your two businesses. You have to give a little, you have to take a little. You have to compromise. You also have to *want* to fit into someone else's life. That's the most important thing of all."

He paused. "Sometimes," he said, "I'd like to find that ex-husband of yours and give him a hard punch on the jaw."

She looked up, startled. "Randy? Why? Why would you want to punch him?"

"I'd like to do considerably more than merely punch him," Chris said grimly, "because he did such a job on you. He undermined your self-confidence. I think maybe part of the problem was that your father had always protected you so much."

"My father did not overprotect me!"

"I think he did, Tory. Out of love. You were all he had. How he must have doted on you! Something I find thoroughly understandable, incidentally. But the thing is, when you went off to college, and later to work in Boston, you were totally out on your own for the first time and you hadn't built up any immunity where people were concerned. If you hadn't been so trusting, I don't think you would ever have fallen for a man like your first husband."

"Randy was simply good at everything he did...like you are," Tory said. "And I... wasn't, especially."

"I don't appreciate the comparison," Chris said. "And I'm not sure Randy was as good at everything as you seem to think he was. I think he built up his ego in part by damaging yours. All that bit about your having two left feet, for instance, and insisting you were a lousy dancer. Once I got you out on the floor, I think I proved my point. As soon as you relaxed, you were great. Once I get you out on a boat and you get over the fear of being seasick, I suspect you'll make an excellent sailor. Meantime..."

Tory waited, and he said, "I'm going to ask a favor of you, Tory. It would sort of prove something to me. I'm going to ask you to let me buy the Pierce-Arrow."

She looked at him suspiciously. "What would that prove to you?"

"That you can take as well as give."

Tory stood suddenly, and walked over to the table where she'd left her handbag earlier. She fished around inside it, and came up with the keys to the Pierce. "Here," she said, going to Chris and handing the keys to him.

He stared down at the keys without taking them. "They belong to the Pierce?"

"Yes."

"Then you're going to sell her to me?"

"No," Tory said, "I'm going to give her to you."

Chris rocked back on his heels. "You," he said, "are out of your mind."

"Why?"

"You need the money, dammit. This isn't the moment for you to make a quixotic gesture."

"I'm not making a quixotic gesture. I want to give you the Pierce. I sincerely mean that. And I'll make out, regardless. I have other cars to restore, and will have still more. So if you want the Pierce, it's yours."

"What about you?" he demanded roughly. "If I want you, are you mine, too?"

Suddenly Tory's mouth quivered, and her eyes filled with tears. "It isn't that simple," she said.

Chris got to his feet, contrition stamped on his features. But as much as he wanted to reach out to Tory, he kept his hands at his side as he asked, "Why isn't it that simple?"

"Because whatever you say, you're you and I'm me. How could I possibly live your life? How could you possibly live mine? Just as one example, how could I ever possibly preside in your homes, be your hostess?"

Chris grinned. "Are you proposing to me, Victoria Morgan?" he asked her.

Tory flushed, and instinctively turned away. Chris's hand shot out, detaining her. "You don't have to answer that question," he said, "but I'll answer yours. I think you'd make the loveliest hostess a man could ever have. Though I'm not that keen on large-scale entertaining, there are times, I admit, when I need to put on a show of sorts. And it would be an awful lot easier with you by my side.

"As to how I could fit into your life, I told you I've been thinking lately that I work too hard. I've brought a lot of good people into the company, people I can trust to take over some of the load. For a long time, I've wanted to do more designing and there have been so many other things occupying my attention I just haven't been able to. So as far as I'm concerned, I could move into your house here, if that's what you'd like, or we could move into mine, or get another house in Chatham. I presume you'd want to live in Chatham."

"I honestly don't think you know what you're saying, Chris."

"Ah, but I do, Tory," Chris told her. "I've been practicing what I'm saying for quite a while now. But I couldn't say it until I knew my eyes were all right, and until Gus Burke was behind bars. Why do you think I didn't want you to come to Boston with me when I went into the hospital? I was afraid Burke might follow. That's why I stayed up there instead of coming back to Chatham. That's why I went to Essex. I was trying to get Burke on *my* trail because I wanted him a million miles away from you...."

"Suppose your eyes weren't all right?" Tory asked him.

"Are you asking me if I think you'd have walked out on me?" Chris shook his head. "No. I knew I could count on you, whatever the outcome. I knew you'd stay with me through darkness as well as through light. I'm right about that, am I not?''

Moved, Tory averted her head. And because she had to change the subject, if only slightly, she said, "Why did you say you know I'd want to live in Chatham?''

"Because of the garage, I suppose," Chris said. "Your underground garage. We could duplicate it somewhere else but something tells me that you like the place you have.''

She stared at him puzzled. "Are you saying," she asked, "that if I were..."

"If you were what, Tory?''

She stumbled on the words. "If I were your... wife... you'd have no objection to my still restoring antique cars?''

"Why should I have?" Chris paused. "Though I'd as soon you gave up the limo service," he admitted. "It would be nice to have you working just one instead of two jobs, so I could see that much more of you.''

"I suppose my car restoration would be considered a hobby.''

Chris laughed. "No way," he assured her. "I *am* a good businessman, Tory. I'd expect you to make a profit.''

His eyes roamed around her living room. "I like this house," he said. "My Monet, incidentally, would look great over your mantel. And there'd be plenty of space for a Cape Cod dog to roam around in, wouldn't there? You wouldn't mind having a dog, would you?''

She couldn't answer him.

Chris's eyes caressed her as he reached out and lightly touched her shoulder. "What it all amounts to, Tory," he said huskily, "goes back to that poem by Christopher Marlowe you were reading when you were waiting for me up at the hospital. Usually I'm not much good at quotes, but I'll always remember this one."

He leaned close to her, and said softly, " 'Come live with me and be my love; And we will all the pleasures prove...' "

Tory's eyes filled with tears again. She felt as if she were about to embark on a crying jag. But these were tears of joy she'd be shedding, and she knew Chris would know the difference.

He was right. When you delved deep enough, the surface differences disappeared.

Tory let the tears flow.

*   *   *   *   *

Silhouette Special Edition

COMING NEXT MONTH

#601 LOVE FINDS YANCEY CORDELL—Curtiss Ann Matlock
Yancey Cordell had every reason to be cynical about Annalise Pardee. Yet the fragile new ranch owner inspired a strange kind of loyalty... and evoked something suspiciously like love.

#602 THE SPIRIT IS WILLING—Patricia Coughlin
Thrust into an out-of-body experience, Jason Allaire landed the unlikely role of guardian angel to adorable oddball Maxi Love. But would earthy masculine urges topple his halo and destroy his second chance at love?

#603 SHOWDOWN AT SIN CREEK—Jessica St. James
LaRue Tate wasn't about to let the government commandeer her precious prairieland. But when "government" fleshed out as handsome, rakish J. B. Rafferty, she faced an unexpected showdown—with her own bridling passions!

#604 GALAHAD'S BRIDE—Ada Steward
Horseman Houston Carder had a heart the size of Texas, with more than enough room for sheltering delicate Laura Warner. But this particular damsel seemed to resist rescue, no matter how seductive the Sir Galahad!

#605 GOLDEN ADVENTURE—Tracy Sinclair
The thrill of being romanced by a mysterious expatriate made it worth missing her boat. Or so thought stranded traveler Alexis Lindley... until she discovered the dashing adventurer was a wanted man.

#606 THE COURTSHIP OF CAROL SOMMARS—Debbie Macomber
Cautious Carol Sommars successfully sidestepped amorous advances—until her teenage son rallied his best buddy, who rallied *his* sexy single dad, whose fancy footwork threatened to halt the single mom's retreat from romance....

AVAILABLE THIS MONTH:

Indulge a Little Give a Lot

A LITTLE SELF-INDULGENCE CAN DO A WORLD OF GOOD!

Last fall readers indulged themselves with fine romance and free gifts during the Harlequin®/ Silhouette® "Indulge A Little—Give A Lot" promotion. For every specially marked book purchased, 5¢ was donated by Harlequin/ Silhouette to Big Brothers/Big Sisters Programs and Services in the United States and Canada. We are pleased to announce that your participation in this unique promotion resulted in a total contribution of *$100,000.*

*

Watch for details on Harlequin® and Silhouette®'s next exciting promotion in September.